195

TROUBLE AT TSA

"We have to worry about getting Ted Briar back before he talks to somebody, particularly somebody like Reverend Ortega . . . An Essential operation like ours can't continue to serve the nation if it ceases to be secret . . . Nemo has got to be brought in."

The secret organization is TSA—Total Security Agency—the clandestine agency of a criminal president.

Nemo is the code name for TSA's top assassin whose awesome ESP and telekinetic powers enable him to perform everything from levitation to teleportation.

The problem: Ted Briar and Nemo have discovered that they are one and the same—And they don't like being used . . . by anybody!

D1359974

NEMO

Ron Goulart

A BERKLEY MEDALLION BOOK
published by
BERKLEY PUBLISHING CORPORATION

Berkley Publishing Corporation
200 Madison Avenue
New York, N.Y. 10016

SBN 425-03395-3

BERKLEY MEDALLION BOOKS are published by
Berkley Publishing Corporation
200 Madison Avenue
New York, N.Y. 10016

BERKLEY MEDALLION BOOK ® TM 757,375

Printed in the United States of America

Berkley Medallion Edition, MAY, 1977

Chapter 1

TED BRIAR screamed.

His narrow bed jiggled him gently and asked, "Another nasty dream?"

Not really a bad dream, no. Not something you'd bother a psychotherapist like his wife's with, or even one of those coin-operated 'bot analysts they have in airport and hotel lobbies. Yet every time Ted had the dream, he fought, breathing hard and thrashing, to get out of it.

Ted sat up, eyes and mouth wide open, and looked around his gunmetal-gray sleeping pit.

What was there in the damned dream to do this to him, two or three times a week lately? Actually it was more a comedy than a horror dream. Ted would be walking down a street in some impossibly pleasant small town in a last-century town, the kind of town which had vanished long before he was born. It was always a warm summer day and he'd be wearing an ankle-length old-fashioned nightgown. Nobody seemed to notice. And he was carrying some kind of heavy suitcase.

The thing was, if he ever delivered that suitcase where it was supposed to be delivered somebody was going to die. That was why he always had to scream himself away from there.

Shaking his head, Ted mumbled to himself, "Don't be stupid." He squinted in the direction of the wall clock.

A thin wire arm snaked up from under the bed, and after squirting two squirts of a liquid, poked Ted's contact lenses into place on his eyeballs. "It's six-seventeen A.M. if it's the chronometers you're trying to see," said the soft narrow bed. "Six-seventeen going on six-eighteen, that's the time."

Ted rasped his tongue over his upper teeth. "Is Haley home yet?" He found he had a strong compulsion to blink.

"No, nope, she's not," replied the speaker mechanism in the computerized bed. "Would you like a cup of coffeelike cereal beverage or perhaps some nice warm soymilk?"

Ted kept blinking, rubbing at his eyes. "What the hell did you spray in my eyes instead of antipollution mist?"

"Golly, I'm not sure. Could it have been, maybe, protein-rich hair conditioner? I'm doing my best, but I really do need a tuneup. You haven't had a house mechanic in for a long time, you know."

2

"We're on the damn waiting list. They can't come till April 22, 2021. Next year."

Another thin metal arm appeared, holding a cup of something steaming. "Sniff this and see if it's coffeelike cereal beverage, will you?"

Ted sniffed. "Nope."

"Listen, how about you go back to sleep for maybe fifteen minutes while I get myself straightened out?"

"No, I never sleep very well the nights Haley's working up at the Dynamo Hill Children's Hospital." When Ted swung his feet over the edge of the bed, his furry slippers came scurrying toward his bare feet.

He'd had the dream even nights when Haley was home. What could be in the damn suitcase that would kill somebody?

"Forget it," he told himself aloud. "It's stupid."

"Huh?"

"Nothing." Ted walked slowly over the pit floor, climbed the ladder up into the earth-colors bedroom. He was a lean blond man of just over thirty, average looking though slightly quirky around the edges. He shuffled across the thermal floor to glance down into his wife's sleeping pit. No, she wasn't there.

You could carry a bomb in that suitcase. No, it wasn't a bomb. It was heavy, but not a bomb. He shook his head, hoping to make the last shreds of the dream fade.

Ted looked toward the draped windows. The

drapes snapped open, pleasant rustic music drifted down out of the main overhead audio speaker. "Looks like another mighty fine day here in Brimstone, Connecticut," announced the house computer. "A brisk, autumnal Wednesday, September 8, 2020. You'll especially enjoy today's predicted temperature of—"

"Who the hell's that guy?" There was an overweight man crouching on the front lawn with a self-operating movie-disc camera cradled in his lap. Ted loped closer to the wide gently curved window to grab up the public-address mike for his lawn area. "Who the hell are . . . Oh, is that you, Mr. Swedenberg?"

The overweight man in the two-piece green travelsuit nodded, smiling sadly toward Ted. The outdoor monitoring system gave his voice a mildly squeaky tone. "I'm only here in the United States for eight more hours this trip," he explained to Ted. "I craved another look. Also, if you don't object, I'm shooting some full-color tri-op to show Mrs. Swedenberg and the children."

"No, that'll be okay," Ted told him. "How's the fishmeal business over in China-3?"

"Can't complain," replied Swedenberg while his camera went on taking pictures. "You're still prospering with the Federal Repossession Bureau Office over in New Westport?"

"Still with FRB, yeah."

"And your attractive young wife, Haley?"

"She's fine. How are Mrs. Swedenberg and the kids? I guess Lars must be in college now."

4

"His name is Nils, and yes, he is," said Swedenberg. "We're all doing as well as can be expected. Fortunately, the starvation rate among the locals in China-3 is much lower than it is in China-2. So Mrs. Swedenberg and the children aren't exposed to as many dead and dying people." He watched his camera scamper over the pseudograss. "We do, of course, still miss our little house here in Brimstone very much."

"Well, your fishmeal company will probably transfer you back to Connecticut someday. Then you'll be able to buy another place pretty much like this one."

"Oh, not like this one." Swedenberg sighed. "There'll never be another Sixty-three Limestone Hills Road, which is why I appreciate your allowing me to drop by now and then when I'm in America."

"That's okay. But listen, Mr. Swedenberg. Haley and I bought this house from you three years ago, right after I started working for the Repo Bureau. I've been thinking maybe you're too sentimental about this place, too attached to it still."

Swedenberg dismissed the idea with a slow shake of his head. "By the way, I hope I didn't scare your friend away. My arrival sent him flying, I'm afraid."

"What friend?"

Buzz! Buzz!

"And I hope his pictures won't be spoiled."

Buzz! Buzz!

"That's the telephone," reminded the house.

Ted scowled up at the speaker grid. "Stay right there, take more movies, Mr. Swedenberg. I have a phone call." He ran, skirting the sleep pits, to the bedroom phone alcove. Sobbing was coming out of there. "Shit," muttered Ted, slowing.

The pink-faced old man who showed on the oval pixphone wallscreen was dressed up as Uncle Sam, except that his shaggy gray beard was stuck under his nose and not on his chin. He was wiping his eyes on a star-spangled sleeve.

"Good morning, Mr. Woodruff."

"Would it make you retch to call me Father or Dad or even Pop?"

"Probably, yes. You're not my father, Mr. Woodruff, you're Haley's father. And your beard's fastened on the wrong place."

"A lot you know about American history and the question of where Uncle Sam's beard goes." Haley's father was calling from a street-corner booth. Outside on the early morning Florida street was parked a landtruck with a huge lollipop of plastic mounted on top. "Where's my little girl?"

"Not here."

"Drove her from the house again with your foul behavior?" Woodruff removed his stars-and-stripes hat. A plastic bubble of bourbon was concealed within the hat. He took a long swig.

"Cheers," said Ted.

"Who wouldn't take to drink with his only girl married to a raving maniac and suffering all the remorse a blighted career can bring?"

"I didn't blight Haley's career. If anybody did it was you."

6

The bubble didn't get sealed quite tight enough, and when Haley's father slammed his topper back on, bourbon squirted onto his scalp. "She had such great potential. Do you know what her 26Q rating was?"

"Two hundred and forty, you've told me before." By twisting and hunching slightly he got a glimpse of the lawn. Swedenberg was still out there. It looked like he was crying, too.

"Where's my little girl?"

"Not home yet, this is one of the nights she works up at the kids' hospital."

"If Haley was happy with you, she'd stay home nights."

"Perhaps, Pop. Why did you say you had your beard pasted on your nose?"

"I'm taking out one of the trucks today, helps me keep in touch." The old man gestured at the landtruck in the background. Emblazoned on its side were the enormous words *Woodruff's Instant Patriotic Breakfast Popps!* "Thousands of schoolchildren all over the South are awaiting the cheerful arrival of a friendly Woodruff truck. I don't suppose, though, you understand a man who has a true calling, seeing as you're stuck in a dead-end job."

"Do all your drivers dress up like Uncle Sam?"

"Some are Abraham Lincoln," said Woodruff. "Tell Haley to phone her poor infirm father soon as she gets home."

"I have to get back to a guy on my lawn who—"

"If only Haley's mother had lived. If only my little girl hadn't left me. If only—"

"Goodbye. God bless America." Ted flicked off the screen. "Don't accept any more calls from that old lush."

"That's no way to refer to your wife's poor infirm father," observed the house.

"If it weren't for him . . ." Ted shook his head, went trotting back to the window. "Hey, Mr. Swedenberg, you saw some guy on our lawn taking pictures?"

"It may not have been a camera. Some sort of instrument, possibly a camera. Is he perhaps someone you hired to do a job for you?"

"I haven't hired anybody to do anything. What did he look like?"

"I think he was a black man. He was very much bundled up for such a lovely autumnal morning."

To his house Ted said, "Didn't you see the other one out there?"

"No, sir," replied the voice of the house computer. "We saw no one except Swedenberg, and he's okay. Anyone strange and the alarms, I assure you, would have gone off."

Ted frowned for a few seconds. "Probably some kind of maintenance man—most of them have electronic immunity." Out to Swedenberg he said, "Well, goodbye, Mr. Swedenberg, nice talking to you." He turned off the hand mike.

Ted made his way to the ramp leading to the primary living room. This way he'd see Haley as soon as she got back from the graveyard shift at the children's hospital.

An olive-green chair met him at the doorway. Ted sat, the chair rolled him over closer to the TV wall. The wall image popped on.

Sprawled corpses, stick-thin, filled the big screen. ". . . and so another small nation, this time Angola, has starved to death. Late last night United Nations observers flew over the capital and determined that less than five percent of the population was left alive." The telescope camera roamed along the dry twilight street, ticking off the dead.

Ted looked away. "I don't like to see stuff like this, not so early in the morning, anyway."

"How do you feel when you view scenes such as this?" asked a jovial, and deep, voice. "Guilty maybe?"

It was Dr. Norvell Perola. This was the show Ted wanted to watch after all.

"Well, chums, I am here to tell you you needn't bother feeling bad," continued Dr. Perola. A giant bald man he was, with an enormous grin and a pair of antique horn-rim spectacles. He was wearing a sleeveless tweed tunic over his one-piece lycra worksuit. "It's not your fault, not my fault, a bunch of illiterate savages can't manage their country. You aren't expected to put the burden of the whole and entire stupid world on your shoulders."

"Yeah, that's right," agreed Ted.

The philosopher was standing in a sunlit field of high yellow grass. In the distance rolling hills, dotted with neat thatch-roof cottages, could be seen. "Here at Utopia East we concentrate on ourselves. That's what my doctrine of Selfism is all about, chums, about finding out what our true natures are, about discovering our true likes and dislikes and then . . . enjoying ourselves!'' Dr. Perola laughed a huge laugh, took a large, hearty deep breath. "Whether you visit us here at our model community nestled in the Massachusetts countryside or simply join me each morning for these talks, the thinking of Utopia East can help you, chums. This morning's talk, for instance, will—''

Buzz! Buzz!

The chair wheeled Ted over to the phone alcove. "I don't want to talk to that cockeyed Uncle Sam.''

Buzz! Buzz!

He picked up the speaker unit. "Hello?''

The plate-size screen glowed on, a freckled man of about the same age as Ted appeared. It was Wally Klennan, one of Ted's few close friends in Brimstone. "Going to have to cancel on our lunch today, Ted.''

Wally worked at the Repo Bureau, too, and they usually had lunch at least twice a week. "What's happening?'' asked Ted.

"Oh, Connie's got the Brazilian flu again,'' explained his friend. "We think that's what it is. Our medgroup android took a look at her over the phone, says she's probably got all the symptoms of that new bug. So I'm going to stay home to give her the shots.''

"Can't your medical 'bot handle it?''

"Robot's broken down again,'' said Wally.

10

"They can't get out to fix it until next April sometime. I'll see you tomorrow probably."

"Okay, give my best to Connie." Ted turned off the phone. He was en route back to the TV wall when the front door wooshed open.

Haley came in. She was a tall, coltish girl of twenty-seven. Dark-haired and pale. This morning her long hair was disordered, smudges of black underlined her wide brown eyes.

"Little late, huh?" said Ted, standing.

"Um," said his pretty wife.

"Don't feel like talking?"

"Oh, Ted . . ."

Getting free of his chair, he went to her. "Something?"

"No, not really. No." Haley shook her head. "Was that Mr. Swedenberg out on the lawn?"

"Yeah." He touched her cheek. "Swedenberg said he saw some guy out there with a camera or some kind of listening gadget this morning. That's sort of odd."

Haley made a small humming sound, saying nothing.

"Oh, and I had the dream again, the thing about the suitcase. I don't understand quite why—"

"You really ought to talk to Dr. Waggoner or somebody, Ted. There's no reason to have a dull dream like that more than once." She exhaled, blinking. "I better get to bed now. See you tonight. Same as always."

"Haley, would you rather be a dancer than—"

"We can talk tonight or sometime." She

11

kissed him once on the chin—her lips were chill —and wandered away toward the ramp leading to the bedroom area.

"Because your father called and he thinks you'd be happier if you were still—"

Her sigh shook her slender body. "He must be doing some heavy drinking again. He always talks about my dancing when he's . . . We'll talk tonight." She went away into the bedroom.

Ted slumped down and his chair rushed to catch him.

Chapter 2

TED turned off the morning news. His car turned it back on.

"The Bishop of Rio," said the unattractive girl newscaster on the tiny dash screen, "is still missing in Brazil."

Slouching down in his contour seat, Ted took a noisy sip from his cup of vitamin-enriched beef-like broth. Outside his landcar it was all trees and sunshine up beyond the two lanes of Stem 33 of the New England Slotway.

"The Bishop of Rio, as you know," continued the tiny red-haired newscaster, "parachuted from a military craft over the Mato Grosso jungles of Brazil late last week. His object was to bless government troops and their United States Military Force advisers who are battling in that embattled section of rebellion-rocked Brazil. So far only his miter and some shreds of his chute have

13

been found. Now here is Ed Skeet via satellite from Rio.''

Gentle furrows formed on Ted's forehead. Why did the Brazilian war remind him of that stupid dream he kept having?

''This is Ed Skeet in front of the Church of Sao Norberto in downtown Rio de Janeiro, where a special mass for the speedy location of the much-loved Bishop of Rio is now in progress.'' Skeet was a tiny, unattractive red-haired man. ''United States Ambassador Plaut was expected to appear but he has since disappeared and it is feared in government circles that he, too, has fallen victim to the dreaded pro-Brazil guerrillas who have unleashed a veritable reign of terror here in recent months.''

Ted switched channels.

''Here, for a change, is a piece of good news,'' said the black newsman on the dash screen. ''The Department of Agriculture announces the price of soybeans has risen only 4.4 percent in the past thirty days. This new increase, while seemingly larger than last month's figure of 2.7 percent, is actually a sign of better times and lower prices. This according to Presidential Publicity Chairman Bobby Bolden, who issued the statement late yesterday from the summer White House in Barbados. Now here's Happy the Clown with today's weather.''

''Forty days of rain,'' said Ted as he clicked off the news once again. ''Leave it off,'' he told the car. ''I'm informed as I want to be for today.''

His dash pixphone made a peeping sound.

When Ted answered his pretty, coltish wife showed on the screen. "Is everything okay, Haley?"

"Yes, more or less. I had a call from Captain Beck and—"

"Captain Beck?"

"You know, Bill Beck."

"Listen, I went out and measured the pseudo-grass again last night. It doesn't exceed the official Brimstone Way of Life Authority height. In fact . . . why's he a captain now?"

"Seems they've changed the Way of Life Authority Team into the Way of Life Patrol. Mainly, I guess, so Bill and his people can wear these skin-tight one-piece sky-blue uniforms with a white stripe all down here."

Ted asked, "Has he got some new complaint?"

"Bill says our cruiserport is leaning."

"It's not leaning. Listen—"

"Argue with him. He reports several complaints about its unsightly list."

"Nobody'd complain about a list—"

"It's okay, Ted, I already called an outfit in Old Danbury. They specialize in straightening up leaning ports."

"But if it's not actually leaning, there's no reason to spend—"

"That isn't really why I called you anyway," Haley said. "I'm also sorry I wasn't in the mood to talk to you when I came home. I'm sorry, really, you're having these bad dreams still. I wish I knew what to do to help you."

"It's something I have to work out," he said. "Don't worry. How did things go at the kid hospital last night? How's little Terry Malley doing?"

"Who?"

"Little Terry. You told me he was having bad dreams, too."

"Oh, little Terry." Haley tangled one finger in her long dark hair. "He slept like a log."

After a few silent seconds Ted said, "We ought to talk more than we do, Haley."

"Sometimes . . ."

"Sometimes what?"

"I wish I hadn't taken that five-year birth-control capsule the day before we got married. We've still got a year and a half to run on the damn thing." She turned her head. "Mr. Swedenberg seems to be back on . . . Ted! That's not Swedenberg. Hold on a sec."

"What?" Ted asked the now empty screen. He could hear his wife asking anxious questions over the public-address mike.

When Haley reappeared she said, "It was a black man, Ted, all muffled up in black clothes."

"Must be the guy Swedenberg scared off. Did you get a good look at him?"

"No. All I can say for sure is he was black and muffled," she said, glancing over her shoulder. "And he was carrying some kind of portable monitoring device. When I asked him what he was doing he ran off."

"If he turns up again, call the cops. Don't go out and try to befriend him or anything. Don't be sympathetic, call the police. Then call me and I'll try to get off work.''

"You don't have to screw up your job over a simple prowler. I can handle it.''

"He's not a prowler if he's carrying around bugging equipment. So phone the police if there's any sign of him again. You might also try to find out why the stupid house isn't giving us any warnings.''

"Yes, I will, don't get upset—''

Beep! Beep!

The car horn was tooting itself.

"Oops,'' said Ted. "Almost at the New Westport Jumpoff. I'll call you from work.''

" 'Bye. Love.''

The slotway shunted him off onto a manual side road. His car's electric engine came back on and Ted resumed control of the machine as it disengaged completely from the NE Slotway.

Was that what was in the dream suitcase? Spy equipment. No, Ted thought, but you're getting close.

Then he blinked, wondering why he'd thought that.

The Federal Repossession Bureau Office complex consisted of seventy-five domed rooms of various sizes, all connected by enclosed opaque ramps. It looked something like a giant sprawl of tangled dumbbells. Ted's section stood out over the mucky waters of the Sound, balanced on pastel-shaded pilings.

When Ted came trotting into his office the handsome, impatient face of young Jay Perlberg was already on the wall of the pixphone screen. "Had a nice leisurely breakfast, huh?" inquired his Skip Division boss. "Lingered perhaps over a second cup of nearcaf with your wife?"

Ted watched a gaggle of sooty seagulls flat-footing around on the sticky sand beneath his office windows rather than look his immediate boss in the eye. "I'm only eight minutes late." Seating himself at his boomerang-shape desk, he clicked on the readers, ID boxes, and mappers. "One of the reasons is that a spade with a—"

"We," the handsome, tanned Perlberg said, "don't care if you're a half hour late, Ted, so long as you—"

"Eight minutes." Tiny faces were rolling by on the screens of the three ID boxes, red Xs were commencing to flash on the mapper maps.

"My main concern is that you're happy," said Perlberg. "Are you happy?"

"Yeah, as a lark."

"Getting along with your wife?"

"Everything is splendid."

One of the desk-top readers commenced talking to him. ". . . Robert Able tentatively located in the Andes Mountains of South America, unpaid for skycar tentatively located parked across the street from a mate-house . . ."

"Okay, I can see you're anxious to make up for all that lost time," said his boss, "so I'll sign off."

"Eight minutes," Ted told the now blank screen.

Another reader, after making a metallic throat-clearing noise somewhere within its speaker grid, told him, "We've tentatively located Leon Rovics at a synthetic-chicken ranch on the outskirts of Burlingame, California. The allegedly unpaid for jetractor is overparked across the square from the local Grange dome . . ."

Picking up an electric pencil, Ted made a notation on a fresh deadbeat chart. "Rovics is pretty good," he said to himself. "Been elusing us since 2018. What with depreciation that stupid jetractor isn't going to be worth more than thirty-five hundred dollars now."

Bleep! said an ID box. A glowing red circle appeared around one of the faces. The crawl had ceased.

Ted squinted at the face. That stuff the bed had swished into his eyes was causing him to see things a little fuzzy up close. "Hey, that's Roosevelt Nixon Thomas, the guy with the six unpaid-for electronic jukeboxes. Do we have a location on him?"

A new red X appeared on one of the mapper screens.

"Tentative loke. Man answering description of Roosevelt Nixon Thomas is employed as a waterski mender in Mystic, Connecticut. Five of the six allegedly unpaid for electronic jukeboxes are supposedly reposing in the loft of an imitation clam-chowder factory in the vicinity . . ."

"Five out of six isn't bad." Ted reached out to punch a repo order on his pickup box.

More faces went rolling by on the ID machines. Then another of the boxes said *Bleep!*

A new face halted on the screen. "Hey, don't tell me he's mixed up with us?" Ted asked.

"This is the notorious Reverend José S. Ortega, commonly known as Rev O," explained a reader. "Long sought by the federal government for a multitude of seditious and near-seditious acts, the infamous cleric has now fallen into our jurisdiction by neglecting to keep up the payments on a stungun purchased from a Gunmartz outlet in Cambridge, Mass., under a flimsy alias."

Rev O was about forty, long-faced and heavy-jawed. A pleasant-looking guy, though. Especially for a deadbeat.

Ted had often seen footage about Ortega on the news. Usually the reverend would surface to commit some antigovernment act or to protest some government abuse. A dedicated man, brave certainly, but somehow not as interesting a person as Dr. Norvell Perola. Ted started a file on Rev O by punching a green button on the edge of his desk.

Bleep!

Something odd had turned up on one of the ID boxes. It wasn't a photo of a face. There was a drawing on the screen, a large pen-and-ink sketch of a vaguely familiar little boy in an old-fashioned ankle-length nightgown.

Ted's eyebrows raised. He said, "Hey, of course! This is what the dream is all . . ."

20

Then he forgot. He could no longer speak. He sat staring at the drawing.

Slowly he fell asleep, eyes remaining open.

After he'd sat that way for nearly ten minutes a door gently opened. This door wasn't where any door was supposed to be.

Someone Ted knew arrived in the doorway. Quietly he said, "Come along, Nemo."

Ted rose up, stepped through the door in the wall.

Chapter 3

FRIDAY morning. Two days later.

Ted had been able to take nearly two pages of notes on Dr. Perola's lecture, uninterrupted, this morning. It was raining, cold and damp outside. The decorative room-center electric fireplace pit kept switching itself on, which sent tiny flecks of black light zigzagging across the TV wall. Not serious enough to interfere with Dr. Perola and what he was saying about Selfism.

"We don't need a lot of stupid books to be happy. In fact, chums, the less we know about the past, the more we know about the future." The giant bald professor was poised next to an open window in his study at Utopia East. It didn't seem to be raining in Massachusetts. At his feet sprawled a plyosack full of books. Bending from the waist, Perola snatched out another book. "What have we next? Giambattista Vico. Stupid.

22

Who needs him?" He flung the book out the window. "What's this one? Benedetto Croce. Stupid. Toss it."

A loud crackling suddenly sounded outside. Ted sat up, asking the house, "What's that?"

"Nothing alarming," replied the speaker directly over his head. "Merely the police making what looks to be a routine arrest."

"On our lawn?" Ted ran to the door. It didn't open for him.

"You sure you want to get involved?" the house asked him.

"Open the stupid door."

On the wet lawn a lanky black man threw his arms high, crying, "Nerds! Fugheaded farbs!"

Two men in blue Connecticut Police daysuits were stalking him, circling closer. Each held a fat gray gun.

The Negro noticed Ted now and tugged his dark muffler away from his mouth. "So you're in with them, too? You're helping—"

Expanding circles of light blossomed from the barrels of the police guns. The loud crackling was repeated.

The black man froze, arms still above his head. Then he collapsed in on himself, arms and legs jerking as he fell down slowly through the rain to splash flat out on the short synthetic grass.

Ted asked, "What the hell did you use on him?"

"Good morning, Mr. Briar," said one of the uniformed men. He was a chubby, grinning man, redheaded and with a face dotted with hollow-

23

center freckles. "Just a routine police matter. You can go back inside and watch your program."

Walking down the thermal path from his front door, Ted said, "Is he dead or what? What kind of guns are those?"

The red-haired man grinned. "I'm Sergeant Nestley. Pronounced the same way as the famous pseudochocolate, although spelled N-e-s-t-l-e-y. My partner is Officer Knudsen."

"This is merely a new type of stungun," explained the thin, blond Knudsen. "The Brimstone police force is giving them a field test this week."

"It's a lot rougher than the usual stungun, from the looks of this poor guy." Ted stepped onto the soggy lawn. Fallen beside the man was a black mechanism about the size of a brick. Ted reached for it.

"Don't touch anything," cautioned Nestley. "Lars, get the med andy."

While Knudsen walked to a hovering blue skycar, Ted asked, "What exactly is this all about, Sergeant? You know, I think this guy was here the other day and he might be a peeping—"

"A little more complicated than that." The freckled Nestley grinned. "I can assure you, Mr. Briar, we'll set everything to right."

"Will we have to testify, my wife and I, or file a complaint?"

"Not at all, Mr. Briar. We have more than enough on this fellow already."

"Who was he anyway?" Ted didn't recognize

the stunned black man. "What was he up to exactly?"

"Standard police procedures make it impossible for me to answer right this minute."

A white-enamel android jumped from the low-hovering skycar. Knudsen led him across the lawn to the fallen Negro. The android bent, with a slight creaking, and scooped up the stunned man.

"Thank you very much for your cooperation," said Sergeant Nestley after Knudsen and the android had climbed back up into the skycar with the black man.

"Could I call the Brimstone police station later to find out the outcome of all this? I still don't quite understand—"

"It would be better if you waited until you hear from us."

"Yeah, but I'm curious as to why this guy was interested in us," said Ted. "I'm not sure what he meant when he yelled at me."

Nestley, chuckling, patted Ted's shoulder. "You'll be doing us a real favor by not talking about this morning's little incident at all, not until we give you an official go-ahead. I can't say more. Well, have a nice day."

Ted stayed on his front steps in the rain until the skycar had climbed away into the gray morning.

When he went in, finally, the hatrack went over him with a hot-air nozzle to dry off his wet lounging clothes. Ted crossed the room, stopping near the TV wall. "Who was that spade?"

Dr. Perola's show was ending, the credits were

unwinding over the closing shot of the giant bald professor at his open window. An unseen announcer said, "The Konnecticut Kable Service has presented Discourse 24 in the continuing series by Dr. Norvell Perola. Viewers who are taking this course for credit are advised to throw away the following books: *Scienza nuova* by Giambattista Vico . . ."

Ted frowned at the front door. Haley still wasn't home from the graveyard shift at Dynamo Hill. He really wanted to talk to her, about the black man and what had happened.

The door opened. Haley came in. The shadows under her eyes were deeper, the short skirt of her tan lycra jumper was wrinkled. "Morning," she said, brushing at her hair with one slender hand.

"Later than usual," Ted said. "Things have been happening around—"

"Oh, Ted." Haley beckoned a chair over, lowered herself into it, and let her long legs spread wide. "I'm not up to conversation right yet."

"Okay, so listen, then. You know that Negro guy who was skulking around the other day? Two cops were here a few minutes ago, they grabbed the guy. Before they grabbed him they—"

"Let's wait and talk when you get home from work." Haley kicked off her shoes. "We had a lot of extra emergencies at the hospital last night. I'm extra tired."

"They shot this guy with some new kind of stungun. It knocked him right over."

Haley bounced up, made her way to the sleepingroom ramp. "We'll have lots of time tonight, save it for then. I am interested, but not now, Ted.''

"We won't have any time tonight," he reminded her. "This is our weekly TF session night. At the Jakesens' tonight."

"Well, I'll call you at work." She headed up the ramp. "Better start letting the house get you ready. Jay's getting very concerned about your being late."

"Huh?"

His wife turned away. "I said Mr. Perlberg probably, from what you've told me, won't like you to be late again. See you tonight." She left the room.

Ted stood watching the door she'd gone through. After a moment he turned himself over to the house.

Chapter 4

"THERE must have been fifty of them at least
. . . what am I saying? I read the body-count
report afterward. There were fifty-six of the little
nerds living in this defunct sector of Bridgeport.
All different kinds . . . fox terriers, collies,
foxhounds, schnauzers, beagles, sheepdogs
. . . So we came in low over this side street where
they were foraging. I'm piloting the skycar and
Rick Marshall . . . You know Marshall, don't all
of you? Cyborg, he and his wife live over in
Redding. Rick is on the deathray. Okay, so we
come in at about a hundred feet and I tip Rick
the—"

"Dead dogs," said Jessica Jakesen. "All I
ever hear is dead dogs. When it isn't dead dogs,
it's dead cats. Once last week it was dead
monkeys."

"Oh, yeah, did I tell all of you about that?" Bruce Jakesen asked the rest of them in his wide, circular living room. "Seems there were a couple dozen . . . What am I saying? The body-count report gave the total as twenty-seven. Okay, there were twenty-seven of these little farbs living in what used to be called the Bronx. Any of you ever hear of the Bronx? Okay, so we come in low over—"

"Ahum. Ahum." The Jakesens' robot bar had rolled into the center of the room, a cylindrical mechanism, highly polished. "I am prepared to serve a second, and final, round of drinks before the evening's True-False MechanoTherapy session starts."

"Another nearvodka," said Haley.

Douglas Fine lit a fresh celery-cig, coughed, and said, "Double pseudobourbon on ice."

His wife, Dory, wrinkled her nose. "Nothing more, thanks."

Ted shook his head. "Nope, nothing for me either." The first one had hit him unexpectedly hard.

Cuz McAlpin said, "The same as before, make it a double."

Wally Klennan said, "I guess I'll have just another spruce beer. You'd better not, maybe, Connie, have anymore, since you're getting over the bug."

"Yes," agreed his wife, "I'll pass."

After taking all the orders the robot bar bowed politely and began to make the drinks.

"You guys in ZeroPet," said Fine to his host, "ought to use more re-ams. Lot less risk when you—"

"Zombies," cut in Jakesen, "can't do the work of humans."

"Damn it, don't call them zombies, Bruce." Fine lifted half out of his lucite rocker. "A heck of a lot of my time at RezTech is devoted to getting the public to—"

"Relax, relax," suggested McAlpin. "A weekend at one of our Torchy Bathhouses is what you all need. Then you wouldn't be so compulsive about doing PR for your respective companies every hour of the livelong—"

"Isn't that what you're doing?" asked Haley as the robot handed her her drink.

Glad McAlpin said, "But Cuz does it so pleasantly, with that familiar crooked little smirk of his. You really don't mind."

"Exactly," said McAlpin. "Life is too short to take seriously. Eat, drink, be merry, and visit a Torchy Bathhouse once a week."

"Whorehouse," said Jakesen. "That's what those Torchy setups really are."

McAlpin shrugged, chuckled, accepted a new drink. "Don't care what you call 'em. Long as you visit 'em. Whorehouse, cathouse, bathhouse. That's how I feel about public relations. The important thing is to get our name into—"

"You guys all really feel close to your jobs," said Ted, "really identify."

"Don't you?" Jakesen stood up. "In my case I'm absolutely certain I'm doing a valuable and

30

useful service for our twenty-first-century socie-
ty. With the food supply the way it is, the concept
of a pet is no longer—''

"Propaganda," said Haley. "You aren't telling us what you feel."

"Oh, believe me, he does feel that," said Jessica. "I can swear to that."

"Even so," persisted Haley, hands circling the
glass which rested on her knee, "I believe he's
simply—''

"Almost nine," said Jakesen. "We have to get
going with our TF session. Barney, will you with-
draw now and send in the TF machine, please."

"Yes, sir. Right away." The robot bar made a
deeper bow before exiting.

Wally said, "I didn't know you called that
gadget Barney. Funny namy for a robot."

"Yes, it is a funny name," said his wife.

"Don't start him," warned Jessica, "on that."

"When I was a young man," started Jakesen,
"growing up in the Washington-Oregon Terri-
tory, I used to hang around at a—''

"Save it for the session," suggested Haley.

Ted leaned toward her. "Let him tell the story
if he wants to."

"Why?"

"Well, he's the—''

"No, no," said their host, "Haley's right. No
reason why I should monopolize."

A square man-high mechanism, six-wheeled,
came gliding into their midst. It was a gunmetal
color, its front rich with dials, gauges, and tiny
lights. "Everybody ready for another self-helpful

night of it?'' The TF machine asked. Its talkbox was down underneath it, which gave its voice an odd, echoing quality. ''Then, pray, let us begin.''

A door in the machine's side popped open, several thin wires came spinning out. The ten people in the Jakesen living room each took a wire. At each wire's end was a synskin bracelet.

When everyone had a bracelet attached to a wrist, Jakesen said, ''Might as well get going. Last week we agreed the topic for tonight's session would be childhood once again.''

''I'm really getting tired of everybody's childhood,'' remarked Fine.

Honk! said the machine. ''That's false!''

''Caught you that time, Doug,'' said McAlpin.

''Maybe you'd like to start this off, Doug,'' said Jakesen.

''No, I wouldn't.''

Honk!

''All right, okay, I'll go first, then.'' Fine settled back in his lucite chair. ''I grew up in Canada, as you know. I don't remember much about my early years or—''

Honk!

''Well, there are a few things . . .''

Ted stopped listening closely. He was feeling somewhat groggy. ''Only one drink,'' he said to himself inside his head. ''Maybe it's the drink on top of those antitension capsules I borrowed from Haley. I really feel drowsy. Maybe it's the stupid job. Funny the way these guys seem to love their work, defend it even. I don't feel that way at all. Oh, the FRB is okay, but . . . but what? What else could I do to make a living? When I took those National Job Center aptitude tests right after college they said I was suited for this kind of work. And all those FRB application exams and psych tests confirmed it. Still if that's so, why am I so—"

"Your turn, Ted."

"Hum?"

"We're going counterclockwise tonight," Jakesen told him.

"Oh, yeah." Ted yawned, rubbed at the synskin bracelet. "Childhood . . . the most vivid impression I have about childhood is this . . . is this very peaceful street. The houses are . . . they're not the sort of houses we live in. They're two stories high most of them, square, with big wide porches and shutters at the sides of the windows. It's a beautiful summer day and I'm walking along this quiet, peaceful street. People are sitting out on their porches, dogs are sleeping in the shade of big elm trees. The odd part is . . . I'm wearing this old-fashioned nightgown. Yeah, this old-fashioned nightgown—"

Honk!

"I'm walking along the street, in this long white nightgown, the people don't pay me any mind. Nope, they just go on ab—"

Honk!

"You're telling us a falsehood, Ted," said Jakesen, "according to the machine."

"No, all this is true."

Haley pressed her hand over his. "Ted, you'd better—"

33

"All this really happened to me," insisted Ted. "Oh—and I was carrying this suitcase. Doing some kind of errand for my parents, although they didn't tell me what was in the suitcase. That's odd, too, since they usually—"

Honk!

"Better stick to the rules, Ted," said Glad McAlpin, "or it's not going to do you any good in terms of therapy. When the machine catches you in a lie you—"

"I'm telling the truth."

Jackeson said, "But the machine—"

"The machine's wrong then!"

All at once, the heavy machine shot up from the floor. It jumped nearly three feet straight up, then went slamming down and fell over on its side with a wham.

"Hey!" said Wally.

"Hey!" said his wife.

"Oops, there goes my bracelet," said Fine.

The cords connecting the group to the machine were yanked and tangled by its fall.

Unfastening his bracelet, Jakesen crouched beside the toppled machine. "It's never done that before," he said. "What made it jump like that?"

"Some kind of malfunction obviously," said Fine. "Nothing works right anymore."

"I'll be glad to take a look," offered McAlpin. "I can fix anything."

"What made it jump like that?" repeated Jakesen.

"I did," said Ted. But he said it to himself, not to any of them.

Chapter 5

MORE rain today, splashing down on the gritty beach beneath Ted's office windows, chopping at the gray, scummy water.

". . . positive identification and location of Nils H. Welker, wanted in Texas-2 for being a year and a half in arrears on his solar-roof payments . . . ," one of the desk-top readers was chanting.

Ted watched three forlorn gulls huddled at the water's edge. What he'd done last Friday night at the Jakesens', he still hadn't been able to explain, to account for. "Maybe it really was the stupid machine going blooey," he suggested to himself. "Yeah, but it worked for the rest of the night, once they got it back on its feet. No, I'm pretty certain I did something to it, something to make it jump. I didn't even touch it, though, which doesn't make any—"

Bleep!

"Hey, there's that kid in the nightgown again!"

35

The drawing had appeared, and halted, on one of the ID boxes. Ted stared at it, slumping back in his chair.

After several minutes the door in the wall opened. The handsome Jay Perlberg stood there. Ted had been programmed not to recognize him. "Come along, Nemo," he beckoned.

Ted stood, walked to the door in the wall. There was a gradually slanting ramp on the other side of the door. He stepped across.

Perlberg told him, "A fairly simple assignment for you today, Nemo."

Nodding, Ted followed him down underground.

Agent Joe Roscoe slit the food pouch, sniffed at the sandwich inside. "That at least smells like corned beef," he said. "Maybe you're too young to remember real corned beef, but I sure do. I been after those farbs in the Total Security Agency cafeteria to stock a different brand of fake corned beef for months, and they finally gave in. We'll see what this stuff tastes like. You want my imitation kosher dill?"

"No, thanks," replied Ted. When he was Agent Nemo his voice was a shade deeper.

"Look down there, will you? That's where I used to live when I was a kid, right there where all the smoke is billowing up." Agent Roscoe, a thick-set man of forty-five, was sitting with his legs spread wide so he could look down through the circular observation window in the floor of their self-flying skycar. "Biggest sewage-reclamation facility in New Jersey now, used to be my hometown. There was a deli . . ." He took a bite of his sandwich, thought about it. "Almost, but not quite right."

Ted sat straight in his chair, hands folded. When he returned to New Westport, got back to his desk, he would remember nothing of this trip.

After a few more thoughtful bites of his sandwich Roscoe said, "This whole task this morning is a waste of manpower. Simple little grab job and TSA uses two of their best men."

"Stupid all right," agreed Ted.

"Not going to be much fun either." Agent Roscoe finished up his sandwich. "I'm not saying we have to get rid of some counter-gov farb every time out, but we ought at least to grab something significant."

"Really doesn't make much difference to me."

"Yeah, but you're not career TSA like me."

"Target," announced the control panel of their skycar.

Roscoe peered down between his legs again. "Yeah, there's Princeton. We can start circling Professor Ackroyd's lab."

The ship began inscribing a tight circle through the late-morning sky.

"Never do get used to this part," said Roscoe, shaking his head. "It's a terrific stunt, no matter how many—"

"Quiet until we have the notebook," Ted told

37

him. "You get the box ready." Relaxing slightly, he closed his eyes. "Dr. Ackroyd isn't in the lab."

"No, he's supposed to be at a germ-mutation convention in Pittsburgh, which is why—"

"The notebook we want is inside the wall safe." Ted could see these things, see the professor's windowless cube of an office, the bright orange desk, the safe concealed in the wall. "Okay now, let's get the book."

A few seconds passed, then the red plyocovered book was resting in the palm of Ted's hand.

"You teleks are really . . . Well, back to business." Roscoe took the book, fed it into the copybox next to his seat.

Ding, said the copybox. The original notebook popped out of one slot, an almost exact copy out of another.

Roscoe returned the original to Ted.

Ted rested the professor's notebook on his knee, closed his eyes once more. The book vanished. "It's back in the safe, right where it was."

"Let's go home," Roscoe told the skycar as he dropped the facsimile notebook into an opaque plyosack. "Very smoothly done, Agent Nemo."

"Yep," agreed Ted.

Putt! Prrrutt! Putt!

". . . the star-spangled wienie has to be maintained as a symbol for kids to look—"

"Dad, I think someone's here. I'll talk to you again soon."

"If I'm still alive by then." Woodruff, in a two-piece bizsuit and his Uncle Sam hat, started to sob onto his desk.

Haley said, "I'm sure you will be."

Prrutt! Putt! Prrutt!

"If you'd only kept up your dan—"

" 'Bye, Dad." Haley shut off the call.

The sputtering mechanical sounds welled up, died out in front of the house.

"Wait'll you see him this time," remarked the voice of the computer.

"Just answer the door."

On the themal path was a lanky, feathery-haired man who was hopping on one foot. "I went ahead and purchased the new pair, Haley." He unscrewed his second wheeled foot, replaced it with his indoor foot. Holding the set of chromed, candy-striped feet up, he said, "More horse-power, and better looking, too."

Haley said, "You're sure, Dr. Waggoner, all these new feet of yours aren't some sort of test for me? What I keep wondering is maybe I ought to react more honestly."

Tipped very slightly to the right, her cyborg therapist came into the living-room area. "I debated about these little silver wings sticking out on the sides," he said as he placed the power-feet on the floor inside the door. "A slight bit flashy, yet there is the mythological hint . . . what would you say to me if you weren't being polite?"

Hugging herself, Haley sat in Ted's chair. "Well, you're a splendid therapist, and I guess you're helping me, but people with a lot of different feet unsettle me.''

Dr. Waggoner unscrewed his left hand, dropped it into his pocket, and attached a recbox in its place. ''Good. What else?''

''The identity thing,'' the girl said. ''People with too many spare parts, it's tough telling who they really are.''

''Been talking to your father today?''

''Yes, he called to talk about hotdogs,'' answered Haley. ''He's still threatening to kill himself if I don't come back to look after him. Sales on the star-spangled wienie are down 6.3 percent this month, which always depresses him.''

Dr. Waggoner opened a trapdoor in the seat of his pants, lowered extendable chair legs, and made himself comfortable near the girl. ''The star-spangled wienie is the one which plays our national anthem when you bite into it?''

''No, you're thinking of the gloryburger. The star-spangled wienie is star-spangled. Dyed red, white, and blue, with stars and stripes.''

''Will he kill himself?''

''No, not a chance.''

''Forget it, then.''

''Still he might . . . I'd hate to fail him, too.''

''The way you're failing Ted?''

''Ted's still having those dreams. Do you think it could be because he suspects where I really am nights?''

''Do you?''

Haley shrugged her left shoulder and hand. ''That's not the cause of his troubles, I don't think, but I ought to . . . be able to help him.''

"What's Ted doing meanwhile?''

"Oh, I know, he should help himself, but . . .''
Both shoulders and hands went into this shrug.
"If I didn't worry and preoccupy myself with Ted
and my father, then . . .''

Dr. Waggoner waited for her to complete the
sentence.

Buzz! Buzz!

"I'll let that go,'' Haley said. "Where was I?''

"You remember.''

Buss! Buzz!

"Ought to take this call,'' suggested the voice
of the house. "It's Colonel Beck.''

"Colonel?''

"The Way of Life people promoted him
again.''

Haley tried to keep her attention on the
therapist.

Buzz! Buzz!

After an open-mouth sigh, she said, "I have to
answer this.''

Chapter 6

EVERYTHING smelled of chocolate cake. The smell came pouring out of the scentpipes overhead, rolled along the plasticene corridors of Evriman Center to engulf the customers.

A retired cyborg directly ahead of Ted clutched at his chest with his aluminum hands. "Oy, my allergies," he gasped as he sank to his knees.

Ted ran to his side. "What's the matter?"

"Respiratory complications," gasped the old man. "Allergic to chocolate . . ."

"Apparently the scentpipes are slightly out of whack. They should have it fix—"

"Oy!" The old cyborg stretched out flat on the pebbled floor of the shopping-complex corridor. "My . . . atomizer . . ."

"I'll help you get it out. Where is it?" Ted commenced frisking the wheezing cyborg.

"No, no, schmuck . . . in my finger . . . built in."

"Oh, yeah, sure." Ted caught up the man's aluminum right hand. "Which finger?"

"The red . . . fingernail . . . push . . ."

His bed had sprayed the wrong thing into Ted's eyes again this morning and his vision was fuzzy. The middle-finger's nail looked more or less red to him. Twisting the old man's arm so the middle finger came into the vicinity of his gaping mouth, Ted pressed the tiny button on the knuckle. "Here you go."

A thin stream of black liquid squirted out of the fingertip into the old man's face. "Putz, that's machine oil."

"Okay, sorry. Wrong finger. How about this one?"

Splat!

That was depilatory foam.

"Schmuck, prop me up so I can find the god-damn finger myself."

Ted helped the old man rise to a sitting position. "You ought to have them better labeled. These two both look more or less red, so—"

The old cyborg jerked his hand away from Ted, thrust his little finger into his mouth, and squeezed a knuckle.

"Well, I hope you get to feeling better soon." Ted removed his supporting arm and the old man fell out flat again. Ted hurried on.

"Good morning, Evriman shoppers," said an affable voice from the ceiling. "Our Saturday-morning special in our New Westport store today is neochocolate cake. A big one-half-pound layer cake for only two dollars. You'll find 'em in our

Food Division. Yes, that's exactly what you're smelling right now throughout our vast ten-acre complex. Remember that if you don't like chocolate cake we have a million and one other things for you. As we like to say . . . 'At Evriman Centers You'll Find Something for Every Man!' ''

"Oy," gasped the old cyborg, far behind Ted.

Ted kept moving forward. On the walls glowed hundreds of small clear-wall cubicles, each filled with a sample of a food product for sale.

"I should have let the old bastard lie there in the first place," Ted told himself, slowing. The chocolate smell wasn't so bad here. "What am I supposed to get?" He took his memoball from his pocket, stuck it in his ear.

"I know," said the recorded voice of his wife, "I ought to do the shopping sometimes, Ted, but this emergency came up at the hospital and I'll have to be there most of the weekend. So if you could do it again this time . . . and, please, don't argue with me, because—"

"How can I argue with you? You didn't leave any space on the talkdisc."

". . . tired of Spanish-style food. So, please, don't buy any more tamales, tacos, fritos or—"

"That's Mexican-American-style food. Spanish food would be . . ." An interesting display of foods attracted his attention on the wall. Ted dropped the memoball back away, approached the displays. "What's this stuff?" he asked aloud.

A speaker grid lit up. "Special this week only. Taste-tempting African-style cuisine, based on

44

the stomach-filling recipes of mysterious Angola, where the black culture and the remnants of centuries of Portuguese domination blend to—"

"They all starved to death in Angola," Ted pointed out to the wall. "So I don't see how the food could be very filling or—"

"Keep looking at the estruma," said a feminine voice. A warm hand touched his.

"I don't know which food that is."

"The green soupy business in the red bowl."

Ted chanced a side glance. There was a tall, pretty auburn-haired girl standing next to him. She was wearing one of those new plyosinglets. Swallowing, Ted said, "What exactly did you—"

"Act as though you're telling me something about the prices," said the girl. "I'll, on my side, pretend to be your typical shit-for-brains housewife. Okay?"

"I still don't—"

"Reverend Ortega wants to see you."

"Huh?" said Ted. "Listen, if it's about that stungun, I can't do anything. He'll have to arrange to catch up on the back pay—"

"It's about you. He wants to talk to you about those special talents of yours, Briar."

Ted turned toward her. "Talents?"

The girl smiled at him. "I think I understand what they cost now," she said. "Point at one of the cubicles, Briar. That's right. Reverend Ortega can tell you why you have those dreams."

Ted remembered to point at a sample of food. "How can he know about—"

"Tonight in the park. That's when he can see you."

"What park?"

"Central Park, NYC. Ten tonight."

"New York City? You mean Manhattan? Nobody goes there . . . the whole island is a slum, full of thieves and—"

"Be sure you get rid of your tail before you come." She walked away, mingling with the other shoppers.

How could she know about the dreams? Nobody knew about that but Haley. "Hey, wait."

The auburn-haired girl was a hundred yards away, pushing through a group of part-time nuns.

Ted nudged around a chubby black family, edged through a troop of boy scouts who were stocking up for a bivouac. By the time he got to the nuns there was no sign of the girl. She'd gone off down another corridor, but Ted wasn't sure which.

"I can breathe again," said the old cyborg as Ted went trotting by.

"Good, that's nice."

"No thanks to you, schmuck."

Ted searched the Evriman Center for an hour. He never saw the girl again.

"Nobody," his house told him.

"You certain?" Ted was standing in the living room, watching the twilight spread across his front yard. "That girl could have been lying . . . but she knew about the dreams."

46

"Uh . . . which girl might that be?" inquired the voice of the house computer.

"Nobody, none of your business." Eyes narrowed, Ted scanned the lawn, the shrubs. "You're positive there's nobody lurking out there?"

"Not a soul, no one."

"Check again. I have a feeling there is somebody watching me. I didn't spot anyone at the Evriman and yet—"

"We've checked and double-checked. You don't think your own house would lie to you? That would violate one of the basic laws of robotics."

"You're not a robot."

"The same code of ethics applies to houses."

"Yeah, okay. You didn't notice that spade with the black box either." Ted left the window, wandered around the room. His chair began following him. "Scat, I'm in a mood to pace."

If Haley were home maybe he could talk this all over with her. About who might be watching him and whether or not he ought to try to make it into Manhattan tonight to talk to Rev O.

"She never listens to me even when she is here. She's always up at that damn hospital helping the lame and the halt. A lot she cares about me. I could be lame, halt, and tattooed and she . . . Hell, I'll call her at Dynamo Hill. This is important."

"Is that wise?" asked the voice of the house.

"Yeah, it's wise." He strode to the pixphone.

"A call now might upset the routine of the hospital, endanger the life of some poor ailing little tyke who—"

"Haley's not a doctor, she's only a volunteer." He punched out the number.

"Far be it from me to interfere with—"

"Shut up," Ted told the house, fists clenching.

The speaker suddenly made a loud *awking* sound. Silence spilled out, no further words.

"How'd that happen?"

A smiling medirobot appeared on the phone screen. "Dynamo Hill."

"I want to speak with Haley Briar. She's—"

"Mrs. Briar is no longer working here, sir."

"No, she's there right now. For the special emer—"

"Mrs. Briar has not done volunteer work for us since December of last year, sir."

"Could you have somebody confirm—"

"It's been confirmed," replied the smiling robot. "I'm rigged in with our personnel computer. Is there anything else, sir?"

"No, nothing." Ted put down the phone.

The house remained silent.

"If she hasn't been there nights," he said, "where was she . . . Jesus, am I that stupid? Boy." He returned to circling the room. "Haley off sleeping with somebody . . . my own house bullshitting me . . . Yeah, I will go see Rev O." He made one more circle. "First I've got to get rid of my tail."

Chapter 7

ON the other side of the carhut, that's where they were.

Back pressed against the side of his house, shrouded by shadows, Ted listened. The last of the day was fading, the floating streetbulbs were coming on up above the trees which lined the curving road. Ted couldn't actually see who it was, the carhut blocked his view. He wasn't even sure he could actually hear them when they shifted position. He sensed they were there, though.

Who were they exactly? The cops had grabbed the last guy who was lurking around, and it wasn't likely they'd miss these two. Ted was certain, somehow, there were two of them. The girl in Evriman had warned him he was being followed and watched, which meant this pair wasn't on Rev O's side. Whose side then?

Maybe Haley had hired them, some kind of

private cops. To make sure he stayed stupid and didn't take to following her or finding out where she went when she was supposed to be going to Dynamo Hill. No, improbable. He was the one who should have her watched.

"Who the hell is she sleeping with?"

Could be someone in the TF group. No, she thought most of them were . . .

"Forget about her," he told himself. "You've got to get to Manhattan by ten."

There were still landtrains running into New York, hauling freight, some food and medical supplies. He had no idea what kind of schedule they followed. He'd have to get to the station in South Norwalk. That's where the Manhattan trains were supposed to stop on their way in.

Ted clenched his fists. How was he going to ditch these two? If he took his landcar they'd follow. They probably had all kinds of tracking gear with them. So even slipping away on foot might—

"I spot him first."

"Shit, I going to get hims clothes."

The smoke made Ted cough. The cook fire was made up of branches, pieces of old building, old books. An animal, skinned and headless, was being roasted on a spit over the flames. It looked something like a dog.

Ted was standing on a weedy slope a few feet from the fire. A scatter of dead trees made a backdrop to the cook fire and the six bone-thin boys huddled around it.

"Get hims money, too," said the oldest, a one-eyed Negro of about eleven.

"Sell him," suggested another of the squatting boys. He wore a cracked plyojacket and nothing else. "Sell hims body to meds."

"Shit, no," said the oldest. "After take hims money and clothes, be better sell hims to—"

"This isn't," asked Ted, frowning at them all in turn, "Connecticut, is it?"

"Sell hims head to meds, plenty good shape," said a one-armed Chinese boy of seven, dressed in a pair of running shorts. "Let me cut it off."

Ted had a just-awakened feeling. As though he'd been sleepwalking and ended up here, wherever here was. "Hey!" All at once he realized where he must be. "Hey, this is Manhattan."

"Cut hims balls and dinger off," said the black boy, "put in jar for good luck."

But that wasn't too very possible. You couldn't simply get from Connecticut to New York like that, in seconds, just by thinking about it. That was what he'd done, though. Since it had really happened, that meant . . . what? That he'd been teleported . . . somehow . . . from his place to here. Who'd done that? And how? Something like teleportation wasn't even—

"Me stick him first."

The boys were getting up, moving away from their roasting dog, coming toward Ted, knives sliding out of tattered clothes.

"This has got to be Central Park," Ted said to

them. "Okay. Now where's Reverend Ortega?"

"Shit."

The boys halted, knife hands dropping.

"Who you say?" asked the one-eyed Negro boy.

"Reverend Ortega. Rev O. He wants to see me. Tonight, here in Central Park. Reverend Ortega."

"LP," ordered the oldest, "take him over to the hangout."

"Not cut him?"

"No. Take him there."

LP was the one-armed Chinese boy. He beckoned to Ted with his only hand, went climbing off into the darkness beyond the cook fire.

"Shit," LP complained as Ted caught up with him.

"Something wrong?"

"They going eat that whole spaniel before me get back."

"You guys live on dog meat?"

"Shit, no. That's first dog in month," answered the boy. "Something been killing them off. Can't get squirrels much no more, too. First came here, they had plenty."

"How long have you lived in the park?"

LP shrugged. "Born here, left here."

Down the next slope was a large building, a composite of chunks of other buildings. A jigsaw of brick, wood, neowood, lucite, aluminum, noryl, rusted iron.

"That the hangout?" asked Ted.

LP wasn't beside him. He was running, single arm flapping, back toward the cook fire.

The first room had walls of synboard and rat-skin. A small, low-ceilinged room, not quite square. Illuminated by a twisted lightstrip lamp, which squatted on the dirt floor.

Head ducked slightly, Ted watched a sack-covered doorway. ''I'm Ted Briar,'' he announced to the empty room.

After a silent moment he decided to go through the doorway into the next room. Two hanging lamps provided the light, the walls were surfaced with carton sides and cloth samples. There was a sprung neofab armchair, a barrel, and an altar made out of planks and oildrums. No one in here either.

Ted circled the plank floor once, cleared his throat, sat down in an armchair. He sighed, took a deep breath, the way you do after a long climb. Everything was getting out of control. Haley was . . . seeing some other guy . . . spending whole nights, whole weekends with him. People were watching him . . . mysterious spades, policemen with strange new weapons, pretty girls . . . Jesus, it was all falling apart. Or maybe it had fallen apart a long time ago . . . and he was only noticing it now. But how had he gotten here to Central Park? People simply didn't have powers like that, did they?

Well maybe seeing Reverend Ortega was going to help. Rev O was antigov, but he was supposed to believe in helping people. Sure, traditionally priests were sympathetic, they helped you with your prob—

"That's my chair, asshole." A long, lanky man in a two-piece black worksuit came striding in, a last-century briefcase swinging in his knobby right hand. He was chewing on some kind of cigar, puffing out swirls of smoke.

"Reverend Ortega?"

"I'd better be, Teddy, or we're both in trouble."

"I . . . can you help me? A girl I met in the—"

"You can help me, Teddy. That's the important thing," said Reverend Ortega. "Get your butt out of my chair now. Sit on the barrel, if you have to sit."

Ted rose slowly, watching the renegade priest. "I've heard about the kind of things you do," he said, "and I don't think I want to—"

"Then let's talk about the murders."

"Which murders?" Ted perched on the barrel. "You're always accusing the government of ordering assassinations down in Brazil and—"

"I mean the murders you've committed, Teddy."

Ted stared at him. "Who, me?"

Reverend Ortega laughed, a grating laugh. "That's not much of a defense." Unfastening the buckles of the briefcase, he pulled out a pile of papers and memos. "Let's start with Joao Rebolar. Know him, Teddy?"

"No, I don't, never heard of him. Nobody calls me Teddy, by the—"

"How about Joseph Sapperstein?"

"I think I know that name," admitted Ted. "Yeah, he was an attorney in Old Hartford, defended some fairly controversial clients. He killed himself about a year ago or so. Sure, I remember. It was a suicide."

"Bullshit," said the priest. "You killed him, Teddy."

Ted jumped up, took a step forward. "I've never killed anyone," he told Ortega, voice thinning. "You were supposed to have something important to say to me. I don't have to listen to this crap. Talk about killing people, some of these raids you've pulled off have—"

"Sit down, Teddy."

After exhaling through his nose twice, Ted sat again on the old barrel. "I thought you knew something about the dreams. That's why—"

"Ever hear of the Total Security Agency?"

"No. What is it?"

"The government formed TSA about . . . What's wrong, Teddy?"

"TSA. Those initials sound familiar . . . but I can't figure why."

"TSA came into being approximately seven years ago," continued the priest. "It has several functions. One is to keep an eye on people who may be dangerous to the administration, people who are possibly antigov." He laughed his unsettling laugh again. "That includes a lot of people these days. This clandestine agency has also arranged accidents for its opponents, here and abroad.''

"Accidents?''

"Such as the one which happened to the late Joe Sapperstein.''

"The guy committed suicide, jumped off an Evriman tower in Old Hartford. Yeah, I remember the story now. There were witnesses, nobody was anywhere near him when he jumped.''

"You were on the floor below, Teddy.''

"No, I wasn't. We shop at the Evriman in New Westport. I haven't been anyplace near Old Hartford in—''

"Bullshit. You were there the day Sapperstein died, you made him jump.''

"How could I do anything like that?'' Ted demanded. "I'm not a hypnotist or—''

"Same way you made the TF machine jump the other night.''

Ted ran his tongue along his upper lip. "Yeah, I guess I did do that to the machine. But I never—''

"TSA loves guys like you, Teddy. Since it began they've been recruiting certain special types of agents. People with exceptional abilities, people with special powers,'' said Reverend Ortega, exhaling smoke.

"Is that real tobacco in that thing?''

"Yeah, it is. I get them from friends in Latin America.''

"That's going to kill you.''

56

"It'll have to stand in line. And you're dodging the truth, Teddy."

"I wish you wouldn't call . . . Look, I don't have any special powers. If I did, do you think I'd be wasting my time with . . ." Ted began to pace the room. "Do you know how I got here tonight?"

"Tell me."

"This is sort of crazy. But I think . . . well, I was standing by my house . . . you know, in Brimstone, Connecticut. There were a couple of guys watching the house. They aren't yours, are they?"

"No, go on."

"I got angry. Guys watching me, I wanted to get here to talk to you, but I couldn't see how to get clear of this pair. Then, in just seconds, I was standing here in Central Park."

"Teleportation. You know the word, Teddy," said the priest, letting smoke go toward the ceiling. "It's one of your several telekinetic powers. You can move objects, other people, yourself."

"That can't be true. If I could do anything like that I'd certainly be aware—"

"Asshole, they don't want you to know. When the Total Security Agency discovered you had telek abilities, they most likely discovered you had strong moral scruples, too."

"I'm not some kind of prude or—"

"Scruples against killing. With TSA, agents such as you are handled very carefully. They put you into some sort of trance state before sending you out on a job. You're not the only unaware agent they—''

"No, even if they put me in a trance, I can't do any of that stuff. I can't lift up people, move furniture around.''

"Don't try to con me, Teddy, or yourself,'' the priest said. "Quite obviously, once TSA discovered your potential they developed it, processed you over a period of time so you could fully use your latent abilities. They don't want you to know about any of that.''

Ted shook his head. "I don't see . . . Hey, the dreams!'' He stopped still in his pacing. "That's what the dreams mean. I've been trying to tell myself something.''

"No kidding? Fancy that.''

"Sure, and carrying that suitcase around, that's a symbol for these telekinetic powers.''

"Right, and not an especially brilliant one,'' said Ortega. "Looks like your mind's starting to come back under your control. Sometimes happens.''

"Your girl, the one who approached me at Evriman, she knew about the dreams. And you seem to know about what happened at the last TF session in my neighborhood.''

"I have agents planted here and there myself. I'm serious about dumping the Hartwell administration. To me priesthood means a hell of a lot more than simply—''

"How about what I've been dreaming? You seem to—''

"You talked about the dream at the TF session.

You presented it as though it were a real event, but it was quite obviously a dream. A recurrent one.''

"Then you've got an agent in that group of ours?"

Ortega slapped the briefcase. "Do you want to go on being a TSA assassin?"

After twisting his hands together, Ted pointed at the papers Ortega was tugging out of the briefcase. "How many . . . ?"

"How many men, do you mean, have you killed? Fifteen so far."

"Fifteen? Jesus." The breath seemed to spill out of him.

"So, Teddy, do you want to quit or not?"

He had trouble filling his lungs again. "How could I . . . kill . . . how could I kill fifteen men and not even know I did it?" Ted groped out with his hand. Not finding the barrel, he lowered himself down to the floor. "How can I ever . . ."

"Atone?"

"Something like that."

"You can help me."

"Help you how?"

"We're going to stop the Total Security Agency, expose it and finish it. We're going to topple the administration, President Hartwell and all the rest."

"You've got all kinds of information already," said Ted. "You don't need me to—"

"I want somebody deep inside TSA. I want to know a hell of a lot more about them. So you keep working for them, but—"

"I thought you were going to help me stop."

"Stop killing, yeah. But I want you to stay with TSA for awhile, I want the names of everybody inside, I want more information."

"If I keep working as a Total Security agent, they can make me kill somebody again. How can I keep from do—"

"Go see Goodanyetz."

"Huh?"

"He's a defrocked professor. Goodanyetz'll teach you how to keep from going under the next time they want to use you."

"Okay, where is he?"

"He insists on living in the Bronx. I've got somebody to take you to him now."

Ted said, "When TSA . . . when they do whatever it is they do . . . when they process me . . . that must turn on my abilities, too."

"We imagine that's what happens, yeah."

"So if Goodanyetz can work it, I'll be in control of all these telek powers and I'll know it, be completely aware of what I can do."

Reverend Ortega watched him for a few seconds. "That's one of the problems you'll have to face.

"Problems?" said Ted.

Chapter 8

"DON'T you see the cross, you dumb farbs?"

The low-flying skycar was being shaken by intermittent soundgun blasts from below.

"Who's doing that?" Ted asked his guide and pilot, whose name was Casper.

"The cross, you stupid nerds!" The short black young man was shouting into his talkstick. "See it on the ass-end of this machine? This is one of Rev O's skycars."

The shooting diminished.

"Stupid farbs," said the Negro. "A rotten bunch anyway, the Block 26 Angels."

"Some kind of street gang?"

"Yeah, yeah." Casper decided to yell into the mike again. "Dumb farbheaded bastards! You got no respect for the Church?"

The skycar circled, dropping lower and lower, passing over black, ruined buildings.

61

"Too bad you're in a hurry," Casper said. "I could show you my collection."

"Collection of what?"

"Animals," replied the Negro as he brought the skycar down into a rubble-strewn street. "I got the biggest collection in New York."

"You mean stuffed animals or—"

"No, alive ones." The car bounced and rattled to a stop. "I got sixty-eight at our place. My brother and three sisters, we got an apartment building we fixed up over on Block 31. We got fourteen rabbits . . . They're really hard to get, we had to swap six dogs for the last one, for only one rabbit. We got twenty-five dogs, including a Great Dane. You ever heard of a Great Dane?"

"Seen pictures."

"Trouble is," said Casper, unfastening his safety gear, "they got this thing called ZeroPet. Those stupid farbs would love to find our place. So would the Block 28 Angels."

Climbing out his side of the skycar, Ted said, "I thought you called them the Block 26 Angels."

"That's a different gang," explained Casper. "Around here we got the Block 25 Angels, the Block 26 Angels, the Block 27 Angels, the Block 28 Angels and so on. Most of these kids don't have much imagination."

On Ted's right, glowing amidst the collapsed apartment houses, was a white two-story building. Freshly painted, orange light showing through its curtained windows. "Is that Goodanyetz's place?"

"Yeah, him and his mother live there. She keeps him diddling all the time. He painted the whole farbing thing himself, after he renovated it. The Block 27 Angels helped a little, but then they got to rolling the old lady down stairs and—"

"Hands high!" The carved-wood front door had swung inward several inches. A husky old woman in a two-piece overall suit stood there pointing two stunguns at them.

"It's me, Mrs. Goodanyetz, Casper," the black young man announced from the bottom step. "This guy with me is the one Rev O radioed you about."

"What's your name?" she asked Ted.

"Ted Briar."

"That's not the name came out of the radio. The name Reverend Ortega mentioned was Red Dwyer."

"It wasn't, Mom." A plump, pale man of forty appeared next to the old woman, drying his hands with a hot-air tube. "Mother's hearing isn't all—"

"Did you finish in the kitchen?"

"Yes," said Goodanyetz. "All except putting the defroster away."

"You go finish up your jobs. Then it'll be time for social discourse."

"This isn't social, it's political. Now don't go screwing up the efforts of a man like Rev—"

"It's not so good," reminded Casper, "to holler our business out in the street."

"All right then, come on in," invited Mrs.

Goodanyetz. "I don't know why they nicknamed you Red."

"Same way they nickname fat boys Slim," said Ted.

"I thought you were supposed to vacuum the thermals in the parlor."

"Give me a chance, Mom. You said to get the—"

"We'll let it pass. You sit and chat with your friends, I'll finish up your work."

When the three men were seated in the circular parlor, Goodanyetz said, "Mother's really a nice person. It's simply that—"

"Would they like some nearcaf?" She reappeared in the parlor doorway.

"No, thanks, Mrs. Goodanyetz," said Casper.

"How about you, Red?"

"If it's not too much trouble."

"Not at all." To her son she said, "Go make a pot."

"Mom, I have to talk to these two on important business. I can't—"

"We won't fight about it. I'll do it." She left them, to go muttering away to the kitchen.

"We have to get him back to Connecticut before sunup," reminded Casper. "So you got to work fast, Goodanyetz."

The plump man was surveying Ted. "I'll only need a couple hours. Don't worry, once I go to work, Mom usually doesn't butt in," he said. "How long have you possessed psi powers?"

"I'm not sure I do, even now."

"Rev O tells me you teleported here tonight. So you must be able to control at least some of your abilities."

"Not really. What happened was I got mad because a couple guys were watching my house and my wife . . . that's not important. I got mad, the next thing I knew I was standing in Central Park."

"Okay, at least this gives us a starting point. Now, I've seen the file the reverend's been building on you. It seems—"

"Oh my heart! Oh, what pains!" cried Mrs. Goodanyetz from the kitchen.

Ted jumped up.

"Ignore her," advised Casper, who'd remained seated.

"A bid for attention," said Goodanyetz.

Thud!

"She fell over," said Ted.

"She'll get up," her son assured him. "What I was going to say was, you awareness of your abilities seems to be coming closer to the surface."

"Oh, to die like this on my unswept kitchen floor."

Ted glanced at the doorway. "I suppose the dreams have been trying to tell me about this for several months now," he said. "From what the reverend implied the Total Security people have a process for activating all my latent abilities. They don't want me to know about it, though."

"Exactly," said Goodanyetz. "What we'll do is this. I'll fix you up, using a few tricks I've worked out since I left Brainwave Department at Yale-2, so you'll be able to resist going under. Thus you'll be able to recall what happens while you're acting as an agent for TSA and they think you're in a docile stupor.''

''But I'll be able to use all these powers I'm supposed to have, consciously control them?''

''Don't see why not. We'll let them turn your powers on, just as they always have. Only this time you should be in complete control.'' Goodanyetz, slowly, got up. ''Mom's never been quiet this long before. Maybe it really was some kind of attack. Excuse me, I'd better go see.''

''What do you think? Can you?''

''I'm trying, but nothing.''

Ted and Casper were in the skycar, moving across the 5 A.M. sky toward Brimstone.

''Because if you could teleport yourself home from here, I could turn around for home that much quicker. I should take over guard duty in about a half hour.''

''Guard duty?''

''On our animal collection.''

''Oh, sure, I forgot.'' Ted pressed his fingertips harder into his palms. ''Nope, can't seem to do it. Remember, Goodanyetz only taught me how to avoid being entranced. I still don't have any control over—''

''It's okay, don't strain. I really don't mind flying, except I get to worrying about the animals. We got eight chipmunks, did I tell you? They're cute little bastards, chipmunks. I found a book about housepets in the ruins of the big library on Forty-second in Manhattan and they said you can't make a pet out of a chipmunk. But you can. You ought to see them eat out of my hand."

"Next time I'm in the Bronx I'll have to drop in."

"Naw, you won't. You're an okay sort of person, Ted, but you don't have any feeling for animals."

After a moment Ted said, "I guess Mrs. Goodanyetz didn't really have a heart attack, huh?"

"She never does. Shit, she had one of those orlon-noryl hearts put in about six years back," said Casper. "Hey, that looks like your stop coming up. I'll drop down a ways from your house so nobody will spot me."

"Since the reverend's people aren't watching my house, it must be TSA people," said Ted. "Why, I wonder."

"They watch lots of things."

"But how come me all at once?"

"You don't know it's all at once. Could be they been eyeing you for years and you only just tumbled," said Casper, getting set to land. "Don't worry, anyhow . . . Rev O will find out about everything."

Five minutes later Ted was moving, carefully, through the predawn streets of Brimstone. "Stay off the Melmoths' lawn, they've got a whistle alarm . . . Don't cross the Jakesens' landing strip, because of those two robot watchounds . . . Watch out for Doug Fine's—who's that hovering over our back lawn?'' He stopped, ducked behind a decorative tree a half block down from the back side of his house. ''Not the cops. Nope, but I've seen that skycar before.'' He stalked, ducked low, to a nearer tree. ''Damn, that's Jay Perlberg's ship. Sure, there's the glowing JP on the ass-end. What's my boss doing over my back lawn at—Holy Christ! He's the one! He's the one Haley's sleeping with.''

Chapter 9

NAKED and dripping wet, Haley came stomping into the dining nook. "It still doesn't work," she complained.

Ted was scraping black off the underside of his English-like muffin. "What this time?"

"Well, what do you think? The damn cleansing cubicle." She thrust out a wet arm. "The dry hoses aren't functioning, for one thing."

"Don't drip into the neomarmalade, huh?" He slid the jug aside.

"And smell."

Ted sniffed the wrist she held under his nose. "Plant food, isn't it?"

"Yes, I guess it is. It's not body-detergent fluid, but the cubicle squished it all over me." Haley sat down, with a damp plumping sound, in the breakfast chair opposite him. "I really get unsettled when our house doesn't function right,

Ted. I feel as though something were wrong with me personally."

"No chance of anything like that," he said as he took a crunching bite of the overdone muffin.

"What's that supposed to mean?"

"Nothing. Merely light-before-work conversation."

"You don't really care that our house is going completely flooey before your eyes." Haley pulled a plyonap out of the table slot, began patting the damp spots on her shoulders and breasts. "And it's been this way for almost a week, ever since last Sunday."

"Last Saturday." Ted took another bite. "We had the house mechanics in Monday, at special-emergency rates, and they told me they put everything back in shipshape."

"Oh, they could tell you anything and you'd believe them," she said. "The house is obviously still not functioning properly. Here I sit covered with plant food, your cruller is burned beyond rec—"

"It's a muffin."

"See? I dialed crullers for your breakfast." Haley hugged her naked self, began to cry. "My whole world is toppling around me."

Ted stayed where he was. "I'll call the house mechanics again. Meantime, why don't you shower and such up at the hospital?"

"What does that mean?"

"I don't imagine you'd get plant food sprayed all over you up at Dynamo Hill."

"No, Dynamo Hill is a very efficient hospital.'' Haley, still dripping, stood up. ''Did I tell you they're expecting another emergency up there this weekend?''

''Oh, really?'' The overtoasted muffin crackled between his thumb and forefinger. ''So you probably won't be home at all.''

His wife crossed the room to the exit ramp. ''No, I'll most likely be there from this afternoon until Monday morning sometime.''

''House will probably be working perfectly by the time you get back.''

''I wish Captain Beck, or Colonel, or whatever he is, would stop by now. I could tell him a few things about our way of life around here,'' said Haley, taking another step further away from Ted. ''You know . . . Ted?''

''Yeah?''

''Oh, nothing.'' She left the dining-nook area.

''Almost a week,'' Ted said to himself. He hadn't mentioned any of it yet to Haley. Nothing about his visit to Reverend Ortega, and what he'd found out about himself and his abilities. There hadn't been another summons to act as an agent for TSA yet. Ted hadn't mentioned, either, that he knew Haley wasn't working up at Dynamo Hill anymore, that he knew about her and Jay Perlberg. And now she was going to take another weekend off and—

''Time to embark for the Fuh-fuh-fuh-federal Repo Bureau,'' the house told him. Its voice sounded old and tinny.

Ted was pretty certain that, angry, he'd turned off the entire house, using his telek powers, just before heading out to meet with Rev O that night. "Listen, I'm sorry I used my powers to foul you up the other . . . never mind."

"Didn't quite catch that, my hearing hasn't been so hot since—"

"Nothing, never mind." Ted remembered he didn't trust his house either.

"Come along, Nemo."

The wall had opened, Jay Perlberg had stepped into the room. Ted was sitting in his chair, staring at the drawing of the boy in the nightshirt. Now came a difficult part, convincing Perlberg he was in the expected cooperative state. The mental defenses Goodanyetz had planted were successful so far, the triggering picture hadn't worked this morning. Ted remained himself, aware of everything going on. He'd have to feign docile compliance.

"Nemo, come along," repeated the handsome Perlberg. He tapped Ted on the back.

Ted stood up, and without quite meeting Perlberg's gaze, headed for the opening in the wall. "How can anybody go to bed with a guy like this?" Ted said to himself. "He's not bad looking, but in such a conventional way and . . . wait now. Let's concentrate on what's going to happen next, so you can report the setup to Reverend Ortega."

With Perlberg beside him Ted walked down the ramp which curved underground to the Total Security facility. The walls of the corridor were a fog gray, the air smelled of oiled metal and chemical cold and . . . chocolate. No, that must be Perlberg who smelled like chocolate cake. Some new kind of body lotion? Or maybe the Evriman was on the fritz again and—

"I trust your charming wife is well, Nemo, old chum."

Ted suspected the handsome, chocolate-scented Perlberg didn't expect an answer. In this early phase of his Nemo processing he was probably supposed to go along quietly wherever he was taken.

"I'm especially worried about Haley's tit, the left one I think," continued Perlberg as they descended through the twisting gray corridors. "I bit it so hard the other night I'm afraid I bruised it. She kept thrusting it into my mouth, so I felt I had to oblige."

Ted clenched the hand furthest from his boss. He kept his face under control, open and touched with a minimum of expression.

"By now she's sprung this week's excuse on you," said Perlberg. "It's interesting how your extrasensory abilities aren't coupled with any common sense. The average guy would have tumbled to what's been going on long ago."

Ted pressed his fingers harder into his palm. The gray walls continued to unfold. "He must do this every time he brings you down here for an assignment," Ted told himself. "Don't do anything, don't react, don't hit the farbing bastard."

"The way she strokes my schtook when I first meet her, I can tell she believes there's not another one like it anywhere." Perlberg grinned.

"So I'm looking forward to our long weekend down in High World, Florida. Haley's so enthusiastic, all those extra little favors and tricks. Even in an enlightened age such as ours, you'd be surprised how many women still believe all sorts of things are perverse."

The walls changed color. Everything was pale green now.

"If I know Haley, she'll want to spend most of our week in and around the sack," Perlberg said. "But I'm going to High World for more than just good, enjoyable farbing. Haley and I are going to do a lot more than just that. Not that she isn't a damn good . . ."

They reached what seemed to Ted to be a dead end. His handsome boss rubbed the fingertips of his left hand across the pale-green wall at eye level.

Without a sound a panel rolled aside. An enormous room was revealed, brightly lit with floating strips of light. There were desks, huge ID boxes, scanners, a great clutter of complex-looking equipment Ted couldn't identify but which seemed medical in nature. There were eleven people in the room, all seated in scattered chairs and all looking out toward Ted. Four women, seven men, each in a one-piece pale-green worksuit.

"Come in, Nemo," said a round-faced man. "We have a terribly interesting job for you this time."

Chapter 10

HE shouldn't have juggled.

But Ted was feeling somewhat euphoric by this time, realizing all his telek abilities were under his conscious control. When the round-faced technician with the pseudonylon hair pointed at the third, and heaviest, metal ball resting on the lucite table and said, "Now this one, if you please, Nemo," Ted had caused the ball—it was the size of a melon—to float up to the ceiling of the huge processing room. Then he elevated the other, earlier, test balls, caused all five of them to whirl around in a circle in the air, as though invisible hands were juggling them.

The bewigged technician frowned. "What's this, Nemo?"

Ted added the man's blond hairpiece to the whirling balls before bringing everything in for a landing on the table top.

The youngest of the women technicians, Dr.

Hatcher they'd called her, came cautiously up to Ted's processing chair. Lips pursed, forehead lined, the pretty girl began checking over all the wires and cables which had been attached to various parts of Ted. "There shouldn't be any puckishness," she said as she squatted to tug at the coils attached to his legs and ankles.

Dr. Dix, the tall, sad-faced man who apparently was in charge, watched Ted, his head tilted to the right, eyes narrowed. "Are you feeling especially puckish, Nemo?"

"No, sir, not very."

Tilting his head to the left, Dr. Dix approached the complex chair Ted was entangled with. "Do you have any notion why you made Dr. Emerson's toupee fly around in the air?"

"It's not a toupee actually," said Emerson, who had it back in place. "That is to say, I do still possess some hair of—"

"Well then, Nemo?"

"Really can't explain it," answered Ted. He shouldn't have juggled. Nobody down here expected Agent Nemo to fool around.

"Perhaps you feel," suggested Dix, "some resentment against Dr. Emerson."

"Perhaps."

Young Dr. Hatcher had eased around behind Ted to check the wires and tubes there. "Nothing amiss," she announced. "Suppose we continue?"

Dr. Dix's left eye very nearly closed, his lean face drifted close to Ted's. "You've never evidenced any sense of whimsy before, Nemo."

"There's nothing to stew and steam about," said the heftiest of the women technicians, a Dr. Babbs. "Let's unhook the little ferp and give him his assignment. Who gives a fig about whimsy."

"We can't have," said Dr. Hatcher, "an assasin going around snatching off people's wigs."

"It's not actually a wig," corrected Dr. Emerson, "merely a small little—"

"We'll move on to the final steps of the processing routine," said Dr. Dix, stepping away from Ted and the intricate chair. "I'm moderately concerned over this unusual display of whimsicality on Agent Nemo's part. It's probably not serious enough, however, to delay us."

Hefty Dr. Babbs said, "He's about the only little ferp we have available at the moment to handle this particular type of assassination."

Ted forced himself to maintain his relaxed appearance in the chair. They were going to make him kill someone else. The total would rise to . . . "Wait," he told himself, "they can't make you do anything. Not anymore, thanks to Goodanyetz. You've got hold of your telekinetic powers, you don't have to do what the Total Security Agency wants."

He'd been down here nearly two hours, undergoing a series of electronic and psychological processes. Most of them he didn't quite understand. But right now he was in full control of abilities he'd hardly realized he possessed. "All you have to do," he reminded himself, "is go along with them until they've finished here.

When you get sent out on your mission, you pull out before any assassinating gets done. You report to Rev O what went on down here and after that . . . Yeah, what do I do after that?''

Once TSA realized Ted was no longer a docile telek agent they'd . . . he wasn't certain what they would do. ''They sure as hell won't keep you on in the Repo Bureau,'' he told himself. ''You'll be out of a job. What else'll happen? Will they grab me, try to reprocess me? Listen, don't worry so much. Make your report to Ortega. He'll have some ideas about what to do next.''

Dr. Emerson was saying something. ''Don't feel up to the cabinet, Nemo?''

There was a pale-green metal cabinet next to the wigged technician. Ted concentrated. The cabinet rose several feet into the air.

''Very good, Nemo,'' said Emerson as he patted at his synthetic hair. ''Carry it over to the wall and deposit it in front of Dr. Texton.''

Dr. Texton? There were three technicians by that wall, two men and one woman. As Nemo, Ted would have known them all. As himself, though, he . . . ''Easy,'' he said inside his head. ''Let your special talents handle this. Somewhere in my brain I know which one of them is Texton. Relax, relax, and float the cabinet over to . . . there.''

''Very good,'' said Emerson, ''very good.''

Dr. Texton was the woman, a moderately attractive face on top of a very chunky body.

''He's ready for the briefing room,'' said Dr.

Babbs. "You can unhitch the little ferp, Lissa."

Dr. Hatcher went to work on disconnecting him from the chair.

Dr. Dix hovered nearby, hand on chin, watching. "That flare-up of cuteness bothers me, sincerely bothers me."

"Go off somewhere and brood," Dr. Babbs told him. "I want this boy briefed and on his way to Deathless, Florida, with Agent Roscoe by no later than midafternoon."

Deathless, Florida? That was some sort of retirement town down there. Ted had heard of the place. It wasn't more than a hundred miles from High World.

"I'd rather not look." Dr. Hatcher pressed her hands over her eyes, turning her head away from the briefing-room view wall. She was in the seat immediately next to Ted, close enough for her hair to brush at his face.

It was faintly scented, smelling of wild flowers and forest mist. Ted suddenly felt he ought to put his arm around the upset girl. He overcame the impulse, kept his attention on the pictures being shown.

"Nothing but a bunch of old mips," said Dr. Babbs. "We all get old and die, Lissa."

"Yes, and that should be the end of it. Those . . . ugh . . . creatures."

"My very own maternal grandmother lives in Deathless," said Dr. Emerson. "She's just as sweet and jolly as when she was alive."

"Ugh, ugh." Dr. Hatcher rested her head on Ted's shoulder.

Up on the view wall a sun-drenched midday street. The street, curving through the clear air some hundred feet above a shimmering blue lagoon, was itself of a lagoon-blue noryl plastic. Old people were walking slowly along the suspended walkway, most of them in shorts and tunics. Only one of them, a very old man, had a deep tan. All the rest were a pale, bluish white. No one spoke. The only sounds coming out of the ceiling talkboxes were gull cries, an occasional cough, and the rasping scuffle of the old people's shoes on the lagoon-blue pebbled plastic street.

"You're certain your grandmother is pert and lively?" Dr. Dix asked Dr. Emerson.

"She's spry, has all her faculties," replied the technician, "even though she's been dead since 2011."

"They all look . . . fishy to me," said Dix. "This Homan Method still has, I'd venture to say, a few kinks. That woman there, for instance, note how her mouth doesn't quite close and her left arm hangs limp at her side."

"Zombies, that's what they are, zombies." Dr. Hatcher burrowed her sweet-smelling head against Ted's chest.

"Nothing to be afraid of." He ventured to give her hand a reassuring touch.

"So maybe Homan's method of keeping a lot of rich old ferps going after they've kicked the bucket isn't one-hundred percent terrific," said Dr. Babbs. "It's his other inventions TSA is concerned over, particularly the antiplague-detection system. If some ferp on the wrong side down in Brazil got hold of that . . . Nemo!''

''Yes, ma'am.''

''Watch this next section of spyfilm especially closely. Here . . . this is Homan's mansion in the heart of Deathless, designed the house himself. Reminds me of a watermelon that fell down stairs, but they say it's very innovative. Watch the balcony.''

The striped dome had a balcony circling it. A door slid open, a tall, sun-brown old man stepped out onto the balcony and spit in the moat two hundred feet below.

''That's the old blip himself,'' said Dr. Babbs. ''All you have to do is cause him to fall off his balcony into that moat. You can do that with no trouble, can't you?''

''Of course,'' answered Ted.

Chapter 11

AGENT ROSCOE took another bite of his near-beef sandwich. "So it worked, Ted?"

"Yeah, the—oops!"

Roscoe chuckled. "You got to be a little more careful," he said. "TSA might try the same thing on you sometime."

The skycar was passing over artificial, decorative swamps and bayous.

"What do you mean? You're TSA, aren't you?"

"I'm an agent for Total Security, sure. My primary loyalty is to Rev O."

"You're on his side?"

"As much as I can be without getting knocked off by TSA."

"He told me . . . Reverend Ortega told me he wanted a man inside the organization. If he already has you I don't see—"

"Naw, I'm only on the fringes. I don't have a

top clearance. You, though, since they think you're in a stupor all the time, you'll hear a lot more than a C-2 rating agent like me.''

"Rev O wasn't, exactly, telling me the truth when—''

"No, he never lies. A priest can't lie, but he can edit the truth some when he thinks that's necessary.''

"How much truth did he edit out of what he told me? What does he really have in mind for me to do?''

"Rev O wants you to go ahead with this Homan mission. Then you—''

"I'm not going to kill that old man. Ortega promised me—''

"That's right, you don't kill Homan. But you make it look as though you tried very hard. You arrange for the old farb to have his accident, whatever it is TSA recommended, except you pull him out of danger in the nick of time.''

"TSA won't accept that. They think I'm infallible.''

"Most agents slip up once in awhile, even teleks.''

"All right, suppose I do that, botch the assassination . . . what next?''

"More of the same, Ted. You keep right on working for TSA, learning every damn thing you can. In fact, Rev O figures when you're a little more at ease with your powers, you can probably borrow some of the TSA files for quick copying. Same way we got the Ackroyd stuff.''

"Ackroyd?''

"Oh, yeah. You were still Nemo when we pulled that one off."

"Ortega wants me to stick with this, keep working in the Repo Bureau and all?"

"Eventually TSA will get suspicious. You can only botch so many killings before they do. Before they do get wise you should be able to get us a heck of a lot of info."

"I thought maybe the reverend had something else in mind for me. You know, that I'd do this one thing and then he'd help me set up in some new kind of life."

"He's not all that much interested in your life, Ted. He's interested in our country, in the loss of freedom the corrupt Hartwell administration has caused. Your job is to help us get rid of Hartwell and his cronies by exposing him and the Total Security Agency and all the other—"

"When TSA finally does realize I'm not the same old Nemo . . . will Ortega help me then?"

"Well, sure. He'll do what he can, hide you out till the present government is ousted. After that, things will be better all—"

"He'll hide me out? What about my wife?"

"Oh, did you want to keep her? We figured, what with the way she's been—"

"You know about that, too?"

"McBernie, he's the black guy who was monitoring your place until the feds noticed him, got quite a bit of info on what . . . Haley, isn't it? On what Haley and Jay Perlberg were up to while you were out Nemo-ing."

"Right in my house? The two of them?"

"In your house, in your car. Out on the back lawn once."

Ted put his hands on his knees, leaned back in his seat and looked up into the hazy-blue afternoon sky. "And Ortega wants me to keep right on with this, with my job and my life. Everything the same, even though I can now control all these telek powers of mine."

"Your part in the picture is that, Ted." Roscoe glanced down between his legs. "There's the ruins of Disney World. Means we're almost at Deathless. For this job TSA wants us to land and pose as relatives. We get a visitor per—"

"I'm not going to be a part of somebody else's picture. I don't have to do that anymore."

"Yeah, but you have to do what Rev—"

A faint popping sound followed the disappearance of Agent Roscoe.

"I hope I've got everything working right," said Ted. "If so, Roscoe's smack dab in the middle of the Disney ruins now." He lifted the control mike off the dash panel. "New course."

"Yessir, boss," said the voice of the skycar.

"Set me down on the outskirts of High World," ordered Ted.

". . . just the kind of bullshit Hartwell wants you to believe. You know damn well—"

"Nix, nix, Rev O," said the double-chinned man in the three-piece off-white casualsuit. "I want to use this on the 'Family News.' "

The priest sucked in his lean cheek. "That's right, we have to clean up the truth so those

85

simple-minded assholes at your network—"

"It's not me," protested the newsman. "It's the clearance people at Columbia-National. They have, you know, this notion a priest doesn't use foul language."

"When most of my flock is in the gutters, don't expect me to sound like the White House chaplain, Leo."

Leo O'Hearn told his robot video camera, "Stop rolling for a minute, will you? I don't want CN to see any of this."

The camera, which was about three inches higher than him, continued to whir.

"Shit, they send me the stupidest damn equipment on these hazard assignments." He gave the machine a punch in the side. "Stop, already."

"They're afraid," asked Ortega, "I'll smash your stuff?"

"Not you, but the sundry agencies who are after you." O'Hearn had his car to the camera. "There, it seems to be off. When I did my field interview with the leader of the Chicago PeaceBombers, two of my cameras got blown sky high."

"So did the CPB leader."

"I know, I know, Rev O. It's a crazy world, a crazy time to live in."

"No, it's a time like any other time. We happen to have a bunch of crazy assholes running the country. But they can, if we're fast and lucky, be driven out of office. That's still possible in this country." The two men were alone in an office on the eleventh floor of the Empire State Building, the top floor of what was left of the ruined landmark.

"Yes, very well. So let's see if we can get a few minutes I can use, Rev O." There was a pleading tone in O'Hearn's voice. "I don't have to tell you that I myself am in sympathy with—"

"Then give me a half hour," Ortega told him. "Let me go on, let me present the whole case against President Hartwell and—"

"You haven't got enough, Rev O. If you had documentation, concrete stuff, then I could sell a half hour to CN. As it is . . ." He shrugged, then elbowed the camera. "Let's do it. Hum. Surely one of the most controversial figures on the contemporary scene is the underground priest known to his increasing number of followers as Rev O. The Reverend Ortega has been active on the political-activist scene for more than five years now. It was Rev O who dug out the facts about the Little Rock brainwave tests and made them public . . . Rev O and his followers who successfully defeated the late Senator McDermott in his bid for reelection. It was Rev O who saw to it that nearly a half-million poverty-level children in the tri-state area got food when the National Food Bureau funds were being diverted by then Secretary of Food Cundall. Well, the man's accomplishments, though highly controversial, are too numerous to list. This is Leo O'Hearn, somewhere in the tri-state area, and I'm going to be talking with Rev O, one of the most provocative and controversial men of our day . . . right after these messages." He relaxed, grinned at the priest. "That opening went better than the first one, I think. When I pick it up I'll talk to you about—"

"Law!" shouted a voice from the corridor.

"What?" O'Hearn glanced around the office.

"Afraid we'll have to postpone our interview, Leo." Ortega reached into his tunic for his stungun.

"The police are coming up here?"

"Some kind of law, yeah. I'll get back to you." Ortega ran to the window. "And possibly I'll have the concrete stuff you need." He jumped out the window.

"What?" O'Hearn nudged his robot camera, trotted to the window. "Are you getting this? Suicide of controversial cleric as law closes . . . Oh, there was a skycar waiting for him out there. Yep, there they go, clean away."

The office door was smashed open, three plain-tunic men with blaster pistols popped into the room.

"Don't shoot my camera," said O'Hearn.

Chapter 12

ON his way to the floating circular bed Jay Perlberg tripped. His handsome chin clunked against the sexsuite floor, as did his tanned knees and elbows. "Son of a nerd," he muttered. He pushed up, walked three more paces, and tripped again. "What the farb. Now I've lost my hard-on."

"Look around on the floor, maybe you dropped it someplace." Haley was sitting on the round airfloat bed, hugging her knees and wearing the mid-twentieth-century black-lace lingerie Jay was so fond of.

Perlberg got to his feet again. "I don't like jokes in bed, Haley. Or in the immediate vicinity of bed," he said as he rubbed at his elbow. "Save the witty stuff for your nerf-brained husband."

"To be sure." Haley looked not at Perlberg but at one of his reflections in the pink-tinted ceiling mirrors.

The handsome naked man walked away from the bed. He stopped at a one-way oval window. Lights of every color flashed and pulsed out in the darkness. Their sexsuite was in the Nightown sector of High World, where it was always dark. "We're not enjoying ourselves to the fullest," he complained, locking his hands behind his tan buttocks. "We've only had intercourse once since we arrived. You don't even want to order any fetishes from room service." He turned to frown at her. "Want to try the brainstim?"

Haley hugged her knees tighter, resting a cheek against their smoothness. "Nope, but don't let that deter you, Jay."

"No fun by myself." He'd gone over to the twin chairs which floated beneath the electronic-brain-stimulation head pieces on the wall. "You're in a very unconvivial mood."

"I'm always gloomy at night."

"Well, you had your choice. We could have checked into Daytown. Matter of fact, we still can," he said. "We'll miss today's cockfights, but we can catch the last flogging if we—"

"Nightown, Daytown," said Haley, twisting black lace around her finger, "doesn't much matter. It's me, I'm in a gloomy phase. It'll pass."

"Don't toy with that lace, twine and twist it like that," Perlberg said. "You'll give me an erection."

"I thought that was what you were looking for."

"I'm going to use the brainstim first." Perlberg started to sit down in one of the floating chairs.

The chair moved a yard to the right. Perlberg's backside whapped into the floor.

"Jay! What's the matter?"

"Farbing chair moved. Damn, gave me a toothache I hit so hard." He, weaving slightly, got up. Catching hold of the chair he carefully lowered himself into it. He reached up for the brain-stimulation helmet.

The helmet came down to meet him. It whanged onto his head, pressed down until his ears stopped further progress. A huge buzzing and crackling poured out from under the helmet.

"Yow! Wow!" cried Perlberg. His legs went stiff, spreading wide. "Ow! Yow!"

The buzzing and crackling grew louder, a bonging sound was added. Wisps of blue smoke came swirling out from under the chromed helmet, tangling around Perlberg's tanned ears.

"Yow! Yow!" He struggled desperately with the helmet, striving to get it off his head.

Haley had leaped from the bed, come running. "Jay, are you being electrocuted? Is your poor brain being overstimulated?"

"Off, get it off!"

Haley, gingerly, got hold of the helmet and tugged. It left Perlberg's head quite easily. "There you are," she said.

Rubbing at his head, Perlberg asked, "Do you smell burning hair?"

"No, and I don't see any singed spots on your poor skull."

"Lord, that was some experience." He slumped in the chair. "Usually you get pleasant, erotic sensations and images. This time, Lord . . . it was . . . awesome."

"Maybe High World has upped the brainstim voltage or whatever," suggested Haley.

"Awesome," repeated Perlberg. "I was standing on a mountain peak overlooking the entire world and a figure with leathery wings was offering . . . Do you smell brimstone?"

"Nope, only something like hot chocolate."

"That's my new hair-conditioning balm." Perlberg sighed, stood up. "That was really . . . awesome." He inserted a finger in the elastic waistband of Haley's antique underwear, let the band snap against her skin. "Black lace really does . . . Go sit on the bed again, will you?"

Haley complied.

"This time I'm going to do the wild-man scenario, okay? I'll come running at the bed, give a frenzied and lustful animal cry, and leap atop you. Then I'll tear all that frilly black lace off you."

"Might as well."

Perlberg backed across the room. "Here we go!" He rubbed his tan hands together, licked his lips, and started running. A few feet from the bed he howled like a wild man, throwing himself toward the girl.

The bed floated up out of reach.

Thunk!

Chin, elbows, knees plus the ribs on the left side hit the hard floor. The wind went wooshing out of Perlberg.

Haley peered over the edge of the bed. "Jay, did you hurt yourself once again?"

"Yes, damn it to hell. Yes, Haley, I hurt myself." He rose to his knees, massaging his injured parts.

"Why, do you suppose, did the bed move?"

"I don't know. How the hell do I know?"

"Perhaps when you screamed like that you scared it."

"You can't scare a bed." Perlberg tottered toward an upright position. "We've used the wild-man scenario numerous times before and nothing like this ever happened."

"Yes, numerous."

"I better complain to the management. We'll move to another sexsuite."

"This was the last available one, remember?"

"Then they'll have to send in a repair squad." Perlberg surveyed the room. "I don't see the pixphone."

"Phone was right there by the . . . oh, but it's not anymore." Haley pointed suddenly at the mirrored ceiling. "There it is, floating up there."

"This is very odd, decidedly strange," said Perlberg. "I'm starting to wonder if—"

Haley was gone. The air popped, she wasn't on the bed anymore.

"Haley?" He looked all around, saw only images of himself.

Words started to appear on the mirrored wall opposite him, scrawled with an electric pen which had fallen from his trousers earlier.

The words were lettered, large and shaky, one by one. "Leave her alone," the message warned, "or it'll get worse!"

"Nemo," said Perlberg.

Chapter 13

TED came strolling into the lobby of the Daytown Howard Johnson Hotel, hands in the pockets of his new one-piece lycra funsuit, tongue pressed against the back of his teeth to produce a whistle. The three aluminum robots behind the floating check-in desk rotated their heads to inspect him.

"I'd like a suite of rooms," announced Ted.

"Your reservation was made well in advance I trust," said all three robots together.

"My name is Philip Van Horn," explained Ted, flourishing a multicard. "You'll find I have a reservation, I'm sure."

One of the ball-headed robots turned to the reservation box of the HoJo computer beside them. "Ah, yes, here it is. Philip Van Horn of Cheektowaga, New York."

"That's me."

"You wish a normal and not a sexsuite?" the

trio of robots asked. "A man of your obvious savoir-faire and virility ought to—"

"I have some thinking to do."

"Ah, yes, of course."

Another of the robots handed Ted a pseudorubber glove. It had numbers on its palm. "Your key, sir," they all said. "Your room is on the eighteenth floor. That's primarily a masochist floor, by the bye. Would you prefer a sadist floor?"

"Makes no never mind. I'm here to think."

"If you finish your thinking, holler for room service. We feature live hookers, android hookers, robot hookers . . . not to mention fifty-three different flavors of ice cream."

"I'm awed." Slipping on the glove, Ted headed for an up-tube.

There was some screaming going on in the vicinity of the Floor 18 step-out area, a few pained cries of delight. Off in his wing of the hotel, however, a cool silence prevailed. Ted fit the fingertips of the print-glove into the five-hole print-lock on his room door.

"Welcome to your room, sir," said his room. "Today's special vice is bestial fellation, our special ice-cream flavor is fakegrape ripple."

"Silence," Ted told the dangling ceiling speaker. "I want only silence in which to contemplate."

"Excuse it." The speaker blanked off.

From his balcony Ted had a view of one of Daytown's vast beaches. The perennial, artificial sunlight made the blue lagoon gleam. The naked bathers sparkled as they swam and cavorted.

Sitting down on the neotile floor of his living room, Ted asked himself, "Now what?"

He'd thrown a scare into Perlberg, teleported Haley home to Brimstone. He'd used his telek abilities to swipe the multicard from the real Philip Van Horn and he'd jobbed the hotel's computer system to provide himself a reservation here.

"I'm not going back."

Not back to Brimstone, not back to the Repo Bureau or the Total Security Agency beneath it. Not back to Reverend Ortega either.

"Everybody expects me to use my powers to help them out, do something they want. Well, farb that. I'm going to use my powers for me for awhile."

He'd already acquired the suit he was wearing by using his powers. He'd noticed it in a shop display on the Nightown mall when he was hanging around near the hotel where Perlberg had brought Haley. When Ted was a safe distance away he'd caused the suit to travel from the store into his hands.

"And I can get anything this way." He cupped his hands behind his head, allowed his mind to wander. "I can get money . . ."

A wad of cash, over five thousand dollars in large bills, materialized on the floor next to his right foot.

". . . clothes . . ."

Three more raffish one-piece funsuits, including one with an illuminated codpiece, appeared in a heap next to the money.

Laughing, Ted clapped his hands together. "I can have anything I want," he said. "Do anything I want."

He could even bring Haley here, teleport her again, and tell her . . . tell her he loved her and she had to keep clear of Perlberg.

"I won't do that," he decided. "Not yet."

"Naked wrestling?" invited the unclothed blonde girl in the shop doorway.

Ted asked, "Watch or participate?"

"Either." She stroked her smooth stomach. Her nipples began to flash orange and green. "One hundred dollars for the former, five hundred for the latter."

Ted found he was blinking in time with the implanted breast lights. "I'm just window shopping now, maybe later."

"Come back tomorrow, we're having our fire sale."

Ted, dressed in one of his newly acquired suits, continued his stroll along the widest and brightest of Daytown's always-daylight streets. His hand closed around the roll of cash in his pocket, he whistled as he walked.

"MF can save your life," a Japanese android told him as he went by an MF shop with a pseudocherry tree border along its narrow front.

Ted looked down at the andy, who was squatting beside the shop entrance. "I don't think I know what MF is."

"Meditation and Fornication," replied the Oriental android, "good for mind and body, frees you of the accumulated poisons of life today."

"Possibly later. Right now I . . ." Ted straightened.

A huge bottle of beer had just gone by. *Liberty Beer* read the label on the truck-size bottle. The cab of the bottle-vehicle was lettered with: *Woodruff's Patriotic Foodstuff!* And behind the wheel was an Uncle Sam with his gray beard stuck to his left ear.

It's Pop Woodruff, realized Ted. Haley's dad.

"Better to M and F than contemplate revenge," advised the mechanical Japanese.

Ignoring him, Ted hurried on, keeping his eye on the slow-rolling truck.

It swung around the next corner.

When Ted caught up, the mobile beer bottle was parking next to the flagpole on the neat green grounds of the Casanova Middle School.

". . . Woodruff Patriotic Foodstuff wagon is here to serve you, boys and girls, and teachers, too," his wife's father was saying over his truck's talk system. "How can we best fight against the enemies of our country? Why, by being strong in mind and body. Every time you drink a delicious bottle of cold, foamy Liberty Beer you get all the essential B-complex vitamins. When you eat a wonderfully tasty Star-spangled Wienie you get not only good nutrition but a full-color tri-op picture of some famous American of . . . ."

Kids were starting to respond. The doors of a building labeled Dope Lounge were opening and eleven- and twelve-year-old boys and girls were reeling and stumbling out into the warm artificial sunlight. A moment later a gaggle of adults emerged from a cottage labeled Faculty Bordello.

". . . special of the day is our red, white, and blue ham on All-American rye, made entirely of one-hundred-percent pure and nutritious artificial ingredients, containing absolutely no pork or flour or other allergen."

The middle-school pupils were lining up at a window which had opened in the side of the enormous bottle.

Ted sat beside a garbage robot across the street from the place. He rested his hands on his knees, nearly closed his eyes.

Woodruff, weaving and shuffling, climbing out of the cab and made his way to the bottle side. All at once his false beard left his ear to begin circling around his head. Muttering, Woodruff snatched off his star-spangled hat and began swatting at the flying beard in an attempt to capture it.

The beard rose higher, settled on the neck of the huge beer bottle.

"Come back here, you halfwit beard," shouted Haley's father. "This is one step away from being a sacrilege, akin to spitting on the flag." He made a few unsuccessful attempts to scale the side of the bottle.

Meanwhile the nine-dozen bottles of Liberty Beer within the truck all opened at once, began to spurt and foam.

The children tottered back from the window, which was foaming violently.

The beard, flapping somewhat like a bird, flew to the top of the school flagpole and came to rest on the gold eagle.

Shaking his fist at it, Woodruff cried, "How the hell am I going to get you now?"

A communal gasp rose from the kids and teachers as Haley's father left the ground. He floated, slowly, to the pole top. When his rising power left him, he managed to grab hold of the pole.

Ted, whistling, resumed his walk.

A bright sun glowed in the clear blue morning sky, real sunlight it was and real morning. Ted ordered his new executive-model skycar to get down on the landing area on the high roof of the bathhouse. He was over Orlando-2, Florida, having checked out of the Daytown Howard Johnson early this morning.

The words *Another Torchy Bathhouse To Serve You!* were written large in glow-strips across the landing area. The bald android landing attendant had a similar message inscribed on his scalp.

"Best to keep moving," Ted told himself as his ship settled into a roof slot. "Perlberg must have realized by now it was you who caused him all that trouble in Nightown. You shouldn't have . . . never mind. I wanted to get back at that son-of-a-bitch. Yeah, he's sure to have reported to TSA that Agent Nemo is at large in Florida. What'll the Total Security people do? Come looking for me obviously.''

"This isn't a real bathhouse, you realize," said the hairless andy as he opened the door for Ted.

"I realize."

"You'll pardon my saying this, but you don't look much like a man of the sort . . . What I'm getting at is, you seem a man of some integrity," said the android. "A fellow, meaning no offense, of good moral character."

"Well, I'm on vacation," Ted told him. "I want to enjoy myself. I've heard a lot about the Torchy operation and I want to . . . to have fun. See, notice what I'm wearing."

"An oversize funsuit."

"I had to select my wardrobe in somewhat of a hurry," explained Ted. "Still this funsuit ought to indicate to you that I'm here with fun in mind." This was, more or less, Ted's real purpose. His neighbor McAlpin had touted the Torchy Bathhouse chain often enough. Now, to prove to Haley she wasn't the only one who could enjoy herself outside the home, he'd visit one of the places.

"Most of our fun-seeking patrons don't wear such glum expressions, if you forgive my mentioning the fact."

"Well, I'm far from glum. I want the deluxe

treatment.'' Ted crossed the roof to a down-tube.

''They'll fix you up on Floor 6, Mr. . . .''

''Edmund Bierhorst, Junior.'' Ted stepped into the tube.

There were girls scattered all around the step-out. Because of the thick, tinted, scented steam Ted couldn't determine how many girls there were exactly, nor how many were real as opposed to mechanical.

''Welcome aboard. Welcome to another friendly Torchy Bathhouse. Come on over and sit down,'' invited a husky voice.

Ted couldn't see who was talking. He didn't see any empty chairs in the swirling mist either. ''Keep talking, I'll try to find you.''

''The steambath pavilion is a trifle on the blink today. Nothing serious.''

''Allow me to guide you, sir.'' A tall, attractive red-haired girl caught Ted by the hand.

A chair loomed up out of the scented fog, a licorice-color lucite desk was floating next to it. Behind the desk sat a fat woman wearing a see-through bathrobe. ''Welcome aboard, Mr. Bierhorst,'' she said in her husky voice.

The redhead placed Ted in the chair and then was lost in the pink mist.

''You have an interesting voice,'' Ted told the fat woman.

''It's this farbing steam. Gets into my voicebox.''

''Oh, you're an andy?''

''Cyborg.'' She whacked her fat upper arm,

103

causing a tiny door to open. From the compartment within she took a deck of pink file cards. "First off, Mr. Bierhorst, you'll have to sign a release."

"Release?"

"First time in a bathhouse, huh?"

"Well, as a matter of fact—"

"No need to apologize. We need a release to show the United Medical Bureau boys in case you kick off here."

"You mean I'm likely to die?"

"No, no. It doesn't happen very often at all, but we have to play it safe."

Ted brought the form close to his face so the steam wouldn't blur it ". . . 'absolve the Torchy Bathhouse (R) Corporation of all blame in case of my death by misadventure, ecstasy, overzealous . . .' You get many ecstasy deaths?"

"Had an old gentleman in from Madeira Beach last month who went that way. Young lad like yourself, I wouldn't worry."

Ted signed his current alias to the form. "I'd like Mrs. Bierhorst, that's my mother back home in Bridgeport, to have my voxwatch and my—"

"Cheer up, lad, the odds are against your cashing in," said the husky-voiced cyborg. She reached under her desk, slapped her knee, and took a brochure out of the compartment this action had revealed. "If you'll hand over your multicard I'll sign you up for what you want."

Ted began to go through the brochure. "This number fourteen," he said. "Total massage. What is that exactly?"

"A massage."

"Yeah, but what else."

"We rub you all over your body with neobutter, two Norwegian cyborg bimbos with specially built massage hands come in and slap you around."

"I know, but . . . isn't this total-massage designation a cover for—"

"Turn to page fourteen."

Ted did that. "Oh, here we are. 'Kinds of Intercourse You Can Try!' See, I was expecting you wouldn't be this explicit about—"

"Some states we have to be a little coy. Here in Florida we can call a spade a spade. If you have any idea what a spade is. Supposedly it was some kind of shovel which—"

"I guess I'll try number forty-two."

The fat woman blinked. "That's all?"

"Well, for a start."

She plucked the multicard from between his fingers. "Suit yourself, Mr. Bierhorst," she said. "You're absolutely certain you want merely number forty-two? With only *one* girl?"

"One'll be enough," he said, "for a start, anyway."

"Any preference as to the girl? You can get them in fourteen different hair shades, eighteen different body styles, twelve different religious creeds, sixteen—"

"Doesn't matter, although I'd prefer a real girl to an android."

The fat woman snapped her fingers. "We have a new little girl starting in just today. She's a slight bit . . . how shall I phrase it? Inexperienced perhaps. However, she's well-intentioned, lively, and cute as a button. Would you mind—"

"That'll be fine."

She tossed him a key-glove. "Room 6Y."

The red-haired girl reappeared to take him there. "I had you down for a much more experimental sort," she said. "I bet myself you'd go for at least a number thirty-seven, and probably an eighty-one after that."

Ted thumbed through the brochure. "A number thirty-seven? Really? Do you see me as—"

"Here's 6Y. Good luck."

It wasn't as steamy inside the circular blue-walled room. He could see the girl on the bed quite clearly. She was a slim blonde, not more than twenty. Naked, hands pressed against her temples, crying.

Ted approached the bed. "What's wrong?"

Without looking up the girl answered, "I'm never going to earn enough money in time."

"In time for what?"

"To keep the Repo people from taking back my landcar," she said.

Chapter 14

"THIS has got to be him." The shaggy-browed man brought his memo-filled fist down hard on the neowood desk.

The desk cracked across the middle.

"I hate," said Dr. Dix, "to keep cautioning you, Karew, but now that you have metal hands you really ought to curtail some of your more extreme gestures."

J. Edward Karew, District Director of the Total Security Agency, was a large man of fifty-one. Scowling now, he made a short, muttering attempt to get the two halves of the desk top back together. He rumbled across the office. "As I was saying, I'm convinced all these things were done by the missing Agent Nemo. What do you think, pretty boy?"

Jay Perlberg was sitting, stiff and uneasy, in a floating neoprene chair. He'd been watching the stapler slide across the ruined desk top. "Most of the incidents, yes, probably."

"Yes, probably?" bellowed Karew. He swung his free hand angrily back, making a large dent in the metallic wall of this underground office. "You're supposed to be our expert on Nemo. You're supposed to know him intimately, know every little twist and turn of his mind. That is why you've been dorking his wife, isn't it?"

"Basically, yes, though I am very fond of Haley."

"Philip Van Horn," read the District Director off the top memo of his fistful. "Philip Van Horn reported to the police of Iveyville, Florida, that his multicard disappeared from his billfold with an 'uncanny implosive noise.' That was our boy at work."

"Yes, it does sound like him."

"Now we also know this spurious Philip Van Horn spent a night at the Howard Johnson in the Daytown sector of High World," continued Karew. "For dinner he had mockduck, soy patties au pseudogratin, a large serving of homemade-style deep-dish applesub pie, topped off with—"

"Spare us the menus," put in Dr. Dix.

"I'll spare you not a farbing thing." The memos turned to a crackling wad as his metal fingers tightened. "TSA is nothing, Doctor, if not thorough. That's how we've managed to remain so completely clandestine all these many years."

"Until now," said Dr. Dix.

". . . topped off with a foamy carob shake.

Does that sound like something this nerd Briar would have for dinner?''

Perlberg shrugged. "It's difficult to—"

"Didn't you ever discuss his eating habits and food preferences with that skinny wife of his?"

"No, we—"

"Let it pass." Karew consulted the next memo. "A size thirty-eight funsuit, which three conventioning nostalgia vendors swear disappeared right out of a display wall with an 'eerie explosive hum'! Does this ferp go in for funsuits?"

"He might," said Perlberg. "Certainly he's going to act against type for awhile. He's found out, somehow or other, that he is the master of an exceptional wild talent. He's like a schoolboy freed from the drudgery of the classroom. 'No more pencils, no more books,' as the ancient jingle has it, 'no more—' ''

"Doggerel, menus," said Dr. Dix. "None of this gets us any forwarder. What we must do is determine not where Agent Nemo has been, but where he's going to be."

Karew shook his fist. It rattled. "That's exactly what we're attempting to do, Doctor," he said. "We establish a pattern, which will tell us where Ted Briar is going to pop up next. I don't have to tell you, or maybe I do considering you're behaving like a couple of nerfs, how valuable he is to us. Of all the thousands, millions actually, of people we surreptitiously test each year, how many do we find who have any kind of real psi abilities?"

"Roughly—" began Dr. Dix.

"Not a hell of a lot," Karew went on. "And of those we select for processing and indoctrination not even half turn out to be usable Total Security agents." He hit his palm with his fist, producing a bonging sound. "With Ted Briar we've got somebody with a very high degree of ability, especially when it comes to heaving antigov twerps out windows and off balconies from a safe distance. The fact he has these moral scruples isn't exactly a plus factor, but since we can process him into forgetting them when he's at work, it's no big thing."

"I'm wondering," put in Perlberg, "if we're going to be able to turn Ted back into a functioning agent again. This taste of freedom, coupled with his new awareness of what he can—"

"We can process him again," said Karew. "Once a ferp, always a ferp." His eyebrows seemed to entwine as he stared over at Dr. Dix. "It'd be a help if we knew exactly why Ted Briar jumped the slot at all."

"We've never had a case like his before," said Dix, wandering over to the ruined desk. "Now he was evidencing very strong traces of whimsy when we processed him last—"

"Whimsy's not our problem," said the TSA District Director. "We have to worry about getting Ted Briar back before he talks to somebody, particularly somebody like Reverend Ortega. We already know Rev O had that jig watching the Briar place. An essential operation like ours can't continue to serve the nation if it ceases to be

110

secret. You lose the goddamn element of surprise. Nemo has got to be brought in.''

"He's going to be very tough to catch," observed Perlberg. "What he did to me, he can do to anyone we send after him."

"If we intended to rely on force, yeah," said Karew. "What Nemo seems to be doing is kicking up his heels. He's going to have himself a good time for awhile. We should be able, when more facts come in, to predict exactly where he'll be seeking his fun."

"Possibly," said Dr. Dix.

"Eventually this ferp is going to want to see his wife again. So even if we miss him on his round of hot spots, we can nab him when he tries to contact her."

"He doesn't want to have anything to do with her," said Perlberg. "I talked to Haley this morning and she's convinced he's—"

"She thinks one thing now because he caught her schtooping with you, pretty boy. I think something else."

"Granted he may tire of his whoopee-making," conceded Dix, "Agent Nemo is capable of teleporting people, remember? He teleported his wife back home from Florida. What's to stop him from—"

"Trust me," said Karew. "We can use his wife to trap him."

The six votive candles—the one stuck in the plyocup was sputtering—lit up a few square yards of the tunnel. Beyond that it was darkness, damp, and chill. The fifty people huddled on the cracked cement, some kneeling, others sitting cross-legged, were all watching Reverend Ortega.

The fugitive priest stood beneath an ancient *Caution* sign. "What exactly was St. Paul trying to get across when he told us—"

"Roamers!"

Before Casper's warning shout had ceased echoing through the train tunnel Reverend Ortega had produced a stungun from beneath his black singlet. "Okay, flock, you'd better scatter," he told the group. "Which way are they coming from, Casper?"

The black young man had a talkbox held to his ear. "Uptown."

"Scatter downtown then."

The crowd fragmented, parishioners hurrying away into the underground darkness, some of them dropping off the platform onto the tracks.

After extinguishing the candles and packing them in his knapsack, Reverend Ortega joined Casper. "How many Roaming US Police can we expect?"

"Linda says six."

"They know I'm down here?"

"Not you specific, no. They apparently got a tip there's some kind of illicit meeting in progress under Grand Central." He dropped his hand into his pocket, exchanging his talkbox for a stungun.

"Six armed Roamers. We'll retreat." Ortega

took hold of Casper's arm, led him through the tunnel blackness to a metal door. "We'll scoot up this old repairmen's exit stairway."

"We could wait around and stun two, three of them maybe."

"No." He pulled him into the alcove beyond the door.

As they climbed up the rattling stairs Casper said, "We been having bad luck, Rev. The Roamers have broken up two masses in the past week . . . and Ted's let us down."

"He'll be back eventually, and on our side."

"I don't think he's—hey, a rat. Just brushed him with my hand. Have we got time to see if I can catch him for—"

"No, keep climbing," said Reverend Ortega. "It doesn't sound as though the Roamers are going to follow us. Probably went chasing after my unfortunate midtown congregation."

"ZeroPet's got a new ratgas, so it's getting hard to even find a rat anymore," said Casper. "You really think Ted isn't just going to screw around, have some fun with all the telek powers he's got?"

"He'll do some of that," said Ortega. "Then he'll come back to help."

"Yeah?"

"Yeah. Have faith, Casper."

"I got faith in some things and some people, but not much in Ted."

"We shall see," said the reverend.

J. Edward Karew hit the syncaf machine. "I

ordered it without pseudokrim, you farbing ferp!''

Burble!

The man-high machine doubled up as a result of the blow from Karew's metal fist. Neococoa began sputtering out of its side, steam spewed from its top, and little cubes of synsac came clattering out of one of its now-twisted nozzles.

Snorting, the District Director showed the injured machine his back.

A wall panel slid open a few feet to the left of the gasping syncaf machine. ''Oops, hey, am I intruding?''

Karew, eyebrows flapping, faced the lanky young man who stumbled into the room. ''Ten minutes late, Moriarty,'' he boomed. ''I'd just about decided not to give you another chance after all.''

Moriarty, who was two months past nineteen, jumped so the loose-fitting tunic of his two-piece studysuit didn't get caught in the closing wall panel. His left foot hit a spreading pool of syncaf, he came sliding almost up to the scowling Karew. ''I was a little delayed, sir,'' he explained, ''by circumstances. For instance, after I received your summons I had to outfox my parents. You know it wouldn't do to have them let the other side know I've been summoned once again by the Total—''

''What other side, nerf?''

''My father and mother are agents for the other side in our endless struggle—''

''Your farbing parents aren't agents for anything. I've told you that many times, Moriarty.

114

Your problem is you're completely paranoid, which—"

"I wish, sir, you wouldn't use words like farbing when referring to my mother and father. Even though they're clandestine agents for one of the great evil powers in the contemporary worl—"

"Your parents are not secret agents for anybody, Moriarty. You're goofy, is what it is."

The lank young man scratched at his ribs, grinning. "Can't figure, sir, why you try to cover for Mom and Pop unless, as I'm coing to suspect, they are actually double agents. Working simultaneously for the great evil power and for our own—"

"They aren't! They aren't double agents for any two anybodies! Now sit down in that chair there and listen to me, Moriarty."

"Yes, sir. No need to—oops." A spill of neococoa got underfoot and Moriarty went skating across the room into a wall.

When the young man was at last seated Karew pointed a metal forefinger at him. "We have an emergency situation here at TAS," he told him. "I'm putting several plans into operation at once. I'm even going to give some of our less than one-hundred-percent successful agents such as yourself a chance to help out."

"Hey! I appreciate that, sir," exclaimed Moriarty. "I do possess an extraordinary amount of telekinetic ability, and despite all my parents' efforts to discourage me, I'm better at it every day. Why, just moments ago I—"

"The problem we face involves an agent with

powers similar to yours, Moriarty. He may even be as goofy as you," Karew said. "He has decided to desert us, to go out on his own."

"That's really awful, sir."

"It's possible, should all our other plans fail, that a fellow telek such as yourself can capture this wandering agent."

"I'm sure I can, sir. And once I locate him I'll pop him right back here to you."

Karew put his hands behind his back, producing a clang. "I'm confident the plans I'm setting in motion will capture Nemo for us. However, I want you to work on this, too, Moriarty, as a backup."

"His name is Nemo?"

"His code name. That briefing machine will give you all the backgrounding you need."

"Which briefing machine would that be, sir?" Moriarty's gaze followed the direction of Karew's pointing finger. "You mean the pile of scrap metal in yonder corner?"

"I forgot I had a little disagreement with the nerfing thing while I was waiting for you," said Karew. "We'll get another one. Now, you'll be working with another of our extrasensory agents on this. She should—"

"I'm pretty much a loner, sir. On all the other assignments I've undertaken for TSA I've always—"

"Which is probably why you farbed most of them up, Moriarty. For instance, the Professor Allen business where—"

"I didn't exactly screw that up, sir," defended

Moriarty. "Granted the placebo ended up in Yonkers rather than—"

"Never mind, Moriarty. You're going to cooperate with Mrs. Seuss on this," the District Director of the Total Security Agency told him. "She's what you might call a seer, she can predict things. I'm hoping she'll be able to predict where Nemo is, get a vision. Not that we're relying only on her, since I've got the full tracking facilities of TSA mobilized for . . . what is it?"

"Would Mrs. Seuss be a stocky, somewhat masculine woman in her middle fifties, sir?"

"She would. Why?"

Moriarty ran his tongue over his upper lip and then his lower lip. "Well, I saw her lurking around upstairs near the concealed entrance. She looked very suspicious to me, like the mother of a friend of mine. So I . . . well, teleported her."

Karew's fingers made a gritting squeek as he twisted his hands together. "You teleported my seer?"

"Afraid so, sir. Being anxious to test my mettle I—"

"Where?"

"Up near the concealed entrance to—"

"Where did you teleport the old broad to, you peabrain nerf?"

Moriarty watched a trickle of syncarf working its way across the floor. "Only over to Long Island, I think."

"You think?"

"No, no, I'm actually certain." He cleared his throat, making his adam's apple rattle. "Would

117

you, sir, like me to get her back?''

''That would be pleasant.''

Moriarty closed his eyes, clenched his fists, rocked in his chair, grunted, ''Is she here?''

''Not so you'd notice.''

The tempo of Moriarty's grunting picked up. ''Here she is.'' He opened his eyes.

A husky woman with short-cropped gray hair was standing on the floor next to Karew. ''I had a hunch something like this was going to happen,'' she announced. '' 'Ella Seuss,' I told myself, 'you're going to meet a tall young man and go on a trip across the water.' It all came true.''

''I want you to find somebody for me, Mrs. Seuss.''

''That won't be any problem.''

Chapter 15

THE blonde girl let out her breath, dropping the tangle of clothes she'd been clutching to her front. "How did you . . . rather how did we . . . what I mean is . . ." She bent, from the waist, to gather up her fallen garments. "Oh, now I've got mayosub all over my singlet. I keep meaning not to leave the dregs of sandwiches about my lodgings, but . . . how exactly did you get us both from Torchy's to here?"

Ted let go of her arm. "It's a . . . knack I have."

"That is certainly some knack." She began dressing. "I guess if it didn't bother you to see me unclothed at the bathhouse, it won't hurt you to witness my clothing myself. Would you care to look at the bayou instead? One of the advantages of Bayou Village is each cluster of stilt-cottages has its own separate bayou. Sometimes from my balcony I even can see a flamingo, but—''

''Where do you keep your landcar?''

''I forgot about it. That's the reason we're here.'' She tugged a pair of allseason panties up over her hips. ''Car's down in the carpad. The six cottages in this cluster share the same pad, like we share the bayou.''

''You told me there was a disabler on your car, to keep you from driving it.'' Ted stepped over a pile of vidiscs, skirted a plyowrapped half-loaf of soybread, and reached the window of the cottage living room. ''Unless you catch up on the payments within forty-eight hours they'll leave the disabler on until they come and haul your landcar off. Which one is it, that green one?''

''Yes, how'd you pick it?''

''It's dustier and more dented than the others.''

The girl rubbed fingertips over the new stain on her singlet. ''I'm lackadaisical about household routines. Watch out, don't back into the roast.''

''Roast? Where?''

''Under that nonethnic serape,'' she said. ''Did I tell you my name? It's Lang Strayton.''

Ted was concentrating on the car. ''There,'' he said as a small, square metallic box appeared in his palm. ''You can drive it now. I've fixed the regional Repo computer, too. For awhile they'll think you paid up.''

''You did?'' asked Lang. ''You did all that while merely viewing my bayou? Is that the disabler in your hand?''

"Uh huh. They still seem to be using the S72 model down here." He dropped it into a dispose hole in the corner of the room.

Lang shook her head. "This is all very unusual, Mr. Bierhorst." She slapped a plastic hat off a floating chair and sat.

"I'm not really Bierhorst."

"Oh? That was the name they gave me back at Torchy's. I was told Mr. Bierhorst was on his way, you appeared, and when you learned of my plight you offered to help and I invited you to . . . teleportation!" She snapped her fingers. "That's what it is, isn't it? Teleportation. That's what you did, what we did. We traveled from that bordello to here in seconds."

"Yep, that's right."

"I've heard of teleportation, even rumors that there were people wandering around who could do it, but I thought you could only move little things. Such as flower pots and billiard balls."

"I can move those, too."

"But this is much better." The girl's eyes were glistening. "What do you do . . . ? Is your profession going around hunting up nitwit girls such as myself who've gotten themselves into financial binds and are about to have their landcars taken away by the Repo people and have their landlord association bounce them out on their casters and so have to half-heartedly resort to turning tricks to keep body and soul together? Or what?"

Ted picked a synfeather boa and several food-sax from a lucite rocking chair. He seated himself, saying, "I used to work for the Repo Bureau. When you told me you were being bothered by them I decided it'd be fun to help you outwit them."

"Is that one of the qualifications for employment by the Repo outfit, telekinetic powers? I didn't know that."

"Didn't know it myself till the other day," he told her. "My real name is Ted Briar, by the way. I never got around to mentioning it."

"People often have some trouble mentioning things to me, since I tend to talk at great length most often," said Lang. "If I continue at Torchy's that's going to prove a handicap, although my first customer, and the only one prior to you, told me he rather enjoyed my keeping up a steady stream of inane banter, as he phrased it. Seems his wife never speaks at all during their increasingly rare moments of sexual congress. She prefers to remain stiff and silent, lips pressed tight, arms at sides, eyes scrunched tight. That's not much of a way to make love, even in situations where you're being paid. Why were you at Torchy's?"

"I'd heard about the places, wanted to try one."

"You didn't get much of a sample. Besides which, with the steam so thick you could hardly enjoy the decor. I haven't seen much of it myself, although they tell me the place is quite charming and has a wonderful ambience. What now?"

"I'm not sure."

"What I meant was . . . after you teleported

122

me here and saved my car," said Lang, "I feel grateful, obviously. So possibly before I get back to Torchy's we could—"

"You plan to go back there?"

"There's still the rent to pay, plus a few other bills, and, to be frank, your Repo friends are anxious about some other of my belongings."

"I can loan you some money," said Ted. "Unless you really want to go back."

"Not especially, no," said the girl. "I came down to Florida-5 six months ago to forget an unfortunate affair. It was either Florida or moving in on some friends who live up in Black Boston. I selected Florida because I thought they'd appreciate a caricaturist more in these parts. Would you like to see some of my work? My samples are . . . I think they're under the floating sofa over there. You'll have to lift the sofa because the mechanism which causes it to remain floating went bad, as you probably noticed but were too polite to mention since the poor thing is sitting right on its caster there."

"I'll look in awhile," said Ted. "Listen, I can provide you with enough money to take care of the bills and all. After that you can do whatever you want."

"Why me?"

"You're the first person in trouble I've noticed since I . . . since I quit my previous job."

Lang watched him silently for a moment. "You can tell me about what you really did and why you quit," she said. "With the abilities you

123

have, you had to have been more than some sort of repossession clerk. What were you?"

"I was an assassin," he said. "I didn't know anything about it at the time, but that's, basically, what I was."

"Tell me."

He told her.

The day had faded, the bayou was turning a deep blue, the decorative moss on the trees hung black, the flamingo had returned.

"Maybe," put in Lang when she realized Ted wasn't going to say anymore, "you ought to go away someplace, you and your wife."

"Nope." Ted shook his head. "No, she can stay where she is, keep seeing Perlberg for all I care."

"You're mad at her because you were stupid," the girl said. Twilight shadows surrounded her where she sat. "I don't believe she knew anything about your real job. As far as the business with your handsome boss, she made it pretty obvious what she was up to."

"I'm not a detective, I don't have to solve mysteries. Haley's not supposed to—"

"People can do anything. What's important is how you handle it."

"What I know is I'm not going back to Haley now. I don't intend to be a spy for Reverend Ortega either."

"I can understand that. You feel this Total Security Agency's been using you, exploiting you, and then along comes Rev O asking you to do the same thing for his side of the fence. Which is why I suggested—''

"Quiet a minute.'' Ted silently left his chair, eased toward the window. Nearly there, he stumbled over a tin hassock. He fell against the window, head thumping it.

A few seconds later a loud splash came from the bayou below.

Lang whispered, "What was that?''

On hands and knees Ted took a look. "Was a guy out here on your balcony. When I suddenly came hurtling at him, he flinched and went over into the water down there.''

"Somebody's been watching us, listening? A voyeur, you mean?''

"More likely a Total Security agent.'' Ted hunched further down, still watching the oncoming night. "Yeah, there's two more guys pulling him out of the lagoon. Why don't all you farbs go for a dip?''

The two dry secret agents went somersaulting into the air to splash down in the center of the artificial bayou.

"Good,'' said Ted, watching. "Now you join them.''

The man who'd fallen in once was dragging himself toward the edge of the water. He was lifted up, tossed in with his two companions.

"Now I ought to drown all three of them.''

"Ted, don't.'' Lang was kneeling beside him.

"Don't worry, don't worry. I'm not going to kill anyone else. It's only that—"

The living-room door burned away to ashes.

A fresh agent stood on the cottage threshold, blaster pistol in hand. "You can't go dunking our boys in the—"

His gun hand was yanked behind his back. As he cried out with pain he was lifted off the floor, his head thunked against the ceiling. Again and again the agent was slammed against the ceiling. When he dropped to the floor he slumped unconscious.

"TSA's tracked me somehow." He held out his hand to the girl. "Would you like to visit your friends in Black Boston?"

"You mean right now?"

"Right now."

"Yes, fine." She took his hand.

". . . at the pinnacle of a damn flagpole, left there for untold hours to wave in the breeze like Old Glory."

"Should have made you happy, Dad, made you feel very patriotic," said Haley.

"For more than a solid hour no one so much as lifted a finger to help me down. Then the Daytown boy scouts, a hard-drinking, fast-living lot from the looks of them, managed to get me to halfmast," the old man said, starting to sniffle. "Another entire hour passed before—"

"I'm sorry to hear that, Dad."

Woodruff said, "While I was flapping in the

wind, Haley, I had the very distinct impression I saw someone familiar ogling me from across the way. Do you know who I think it was?"

"Benedict Arnold?"

"Oh, Haley, living away from me has made you a terrible cynic," said her father. "No. I'm sure Ted was standing there, smirking like a chimp, enjoying my plight."

"Ted?" Haley reached out, touched the pixphone screen. "Are you sure?"

"Has he run away from you? Has he come down here expressly to do me mischief?"

"When was it you saw him?"

"While I was up the damned flagpole, Haley."

"Was that today?"

"You used to hang on my every word, sit on my knee and hang on my every word, and now you pay little or—"

"When?"

"This morning," answered the old man. "What's Ted up to? Has he quit that dead-end job of his? Has he run off with some floozie?"

"No, Dad, it's the other way around."

"I don't quite understand what—"

"I don't quite either. I . . . well, I guess I love Ted and I just haven't been able to do anything to help him and it makes me so unsettled and angry that—"

"Haley, you haven't done anything your father would be ashamed of?"

She looked at his image on the screen. "No, Dad. No, I'm still your sweet and innocent little

Haley, always will be, and everything is perfectly fine," she told him. "I'm sorry you were up a flagpole. I'm glad you got down."

"If only you'd—"

"Goodbye, Dad." She ended the call, stayed in the phone alcove watching the dark screen.

Chapter 16

"How do you get used to it?"

"I haven't, exactly, yet."

Lang, lips tight together, took in a deep breath. "We're in Black Boston sure enough, this is Soul Food Common," she said. "My friends live off in that direction, along the banks of the Charles." She let go his hand to point.

Ted had set himself and the girl down on a patch of grassy field which was circled with low, narrow cafés and restaurants. There were dozens of them, pressed tightly together. "I'll escort you over to your friends," he offered.

"Yes, but let's walk. Teleportation gives me very odd feelings here in my insides, not to mention the psychological and philosophical questions which arise." She took another deep breath. "This section of town is devoted to research and study in the field of Negro Barbecue, funded by the All-Black Division of the Ford Foundation."

They moved along the row of tiny eating places. *Real Texas Bar-B-Q! We use only 100% Textured Vegetable Protein Ribs! Frisco-Style Ribs! House of Soul Soy!*

"Boston's chopped up into enclaves devoted to the study and understanding of Negro culture and history," explained Lang as they crossed a neowood bridge out of the common.

"Yeah, I've heard."

The blonde girl caught his hand again. "I appreciate your helping me, all these ways," she said. "Do you think the Total Security people will put me on some sort of shit list?"

"It's me they're hunting. I don't think they'll bother you once I move on."

Lang said, "It'll be very pleasant to see Blind Lemon and Cripple Clarence again."

"Your friends are handicapped?"

"Oh, no. They've simply changed their names to suit their field of study."

A line of Negroes was forming outside a barn-shaped auditorium across the street. *See Joe Louis Defend His Title Against Jack Johnson!* proclaimed a lightstrip sign.

"Which is?"

"An old type of black music known as blues," explained Lang. "That's why Blind Lemon and Cripple Clarence live down here in Bluesville. I think, you know, you'll like them as much as I do. You'll probably like Bessie and Ma and Trixie and Ida and—"

"I might," said Ted, "but I've been thinking. We're not that far from Lowell, Massachusetts, so I'm going to head for Utopia East.''

Lang's nose wrinkled. ''You won't like it. Not that I've ever been there, but I have the impression Utopia East is very tranquil and very dull.''

''Exactly right. I need some dull, tranquil place to sit and collect my thoughts about—''

''I should think your recent life in New Westport and environs would have provided enough dullness and tranquillity to last you a—''

''No, now, my life there wasn't all that . . . well . . .''

''Yes?''

''I suppose it really hasn't been much,'' he admitted as they reached the outskirts of Fightown. ''Did I ever tell you about Mr. Swedenberg?''

''No, is he another one of your employers?''

''He's the guy who used to own our house in Brimstone, company transferred him to China-3. Every time he comes to New England on business he makes a special trip to visit our place. He just likes to look at the house. I've always thought Swedenberg was kind of foolish, trying to recapture the lost past. But I realize now the biggest puzzle, though I never admitted it to myself, was how anybody could ever have been happy in our house. Because I never have.''

''You're making progress,'' said Lang, nodding her head. ''Seems a shame to waste your time at Utopia East when you—''

''I've been promising myself someday I'd go there, now I'm going to do it.''

Amplified guitar music, mournful, was filling

the air. There were saloons and bistros all around on the river-front street.

"Blind Lemon lives up above that joint there, Big Mama's. This time of day, though, he's likely to be rowing out on the riv—"

Wham!

The rocking explosion came from the river. A large hydro excursion boat was spewing up black, sooty smoke out of its middle.

"There's Lemon's canoe overturned," cried Lang. "The concussion must have—"

"He's clinging to it," said Ted, pointing. He bit at his lower lip, concentrating on the river.

The damaged canoe, with a long, lean Negro holding to its side, rose up out of the water and came floating through the air toward Ted and Lang.

The growing street crowd commenced making awed and perplexed sounds.

Ted ran forward, fists clenching, furrows cutting across his brow.

The big excursion boat stopped sinking, stayed where it was. The passengers were, one by one and then in pairs, lifted from the damaged craft and deposited on land. No one else moved for several minutes. Then, careful not to get close to Ted, they came to the river edge to the rescued passengers.

Putting his hands in his pockets, Ted walked back to Lang.

"That's quite an accomplishment," said the dripping Blind Lemon. "Lang's been telling me about you, Ted. It occurs to me we could certainly use a fellow who—"

"Uses for me keep occurring to people," Ted told him. "At the moment, though, I'm not accepting any new offers."

"You're really going to that drab Utopia place?" the girl asked.

"I am. Leaving now." He held out his hand.

Ignoring the hand, Lang jumped forward to hug him. "Okay, I hope you work everything out. When you do, look me up. Most likely I'll be here in Black Boston for awhile, or if I'm not Lemon can tell you where I've wandered to."

Ted disengaged himself from the girl, stepped clear of her. "All right, goodbye." He was there, then he wasn't there.

"That's some exit," observed Blind Lemon.

Chapter 17

"I DON'T think," Haley said, "I want to see him."

"This puts me in a somewhat awkward position," said the house. "Since I'm obliged to allow him access whenever—"

"What?" Haley pushed out of the coffeenook, the syncaf splashing up in the cup in her hand. "What do you mean Jay Perlberg has access to our house?"

"Oops," said the voice of the house computer. "Ever since the mister put the whammy on me I've developed a tendency to blurt—"

"What did Ted have to do with this house breaking down?"

The house remained silent.

"Come on," warned Haley, "you tell me or I'll have a repair squad in here and I'll report you to Colonel Beck or maybe even—"

"Perhaps if you allow Mr. Perlberg to enter,

rather than cool his heels without, he'll be able to explain many—"

"All right, okay. Let him in." She strode through the house to the living-room area, slammed her cup down atop a walltable. When the front door opened to admit the handsome Perlberg she was standing there facing him. "So start explaining."

"Good evening, Haley darling." Perlberg took a few tentative steps into the room. "I have the impression you've been avoiding me since you were teleported home from High World. I must say I—"

"How come the house has orders to let you in?"

Perlberg raised his attractive eyebrows. "Beg pardon, Haley?"

"The house, it tells me it's supposed to turn off our security system when you show up on the doorstep."

"This damn computer's been talking too much ever since Ted—"

"You know about that, too?"

Perlberg went two careful steps nearer to the angry girl. "I'm certain, Haley darling," he said, "I explained to you your husband possesses certain unusual abilities. We've established beyond a doubt it was Ted who was at High World the same time you and I were sharing our exciting weekend—"

"You already told me Ted had telekinetic powers."

"Well, he'd have to, wouldn't he? To toss me around in such an embarrassing way? To transport, to teleport actually, you back here the way he did?"

"But you won't tell me how he all of a sudden developed such powers and why, when he found out the terrible things I was doing, he—"

"Really, Haley darling, ours has been a wonderful relationship. Not at all terr—"

"You know a hell of a lot more about Ted than you've told me," Haley accused. "You probably even know where he is, why he hasn't come home."

Perlberg asked, "You really don't have any notion where he is?"

"I imagine he's left me, not that I blame him. That's all I know."

"You've really, Haley darling, got to stop talking about our relationship as though it were some sinful episode. This is the twenty-first century after all, marriage is by no means a solemn contract which—"

"There's something else going on. The Repo Bureau wouldn't . . ." She shrugged. "You're involved, you and Ted, in something much more complex than repossession, Jay."

Perlberg attempted a smile. "Haley, darling, I can assure you—"

"Do you know where he is?"

"They wouldn't have sent me to you if I knew that."

"They? Who do you mean?"

Making an annoyed tisking sound, Perlberg said, "There was a hope in my heart, Haley darling, I wouldn't have to do this." From inside the jacket of his three-piece casualsuit he took a small stungun.

The gun buzzed, Haley stiffened, then collapsed to the floor with a bouncing thump.

"She's never going to like me after this," Perlberg said to the men who came into the house.

One of them was Karew. "We'll fix it so she won't even remember you were here, pretty boy."

"Shooting one's friends," murmured Perlberg, while slowly putting his stungun back in its place, "isn't the sort of thing I rel—"

"It's a mug's game we're in." Karew pointed a thumb at the fallen girl, ordering two of the men, "Pick her up and toss her on that floating sofa. Can you work there, Doc?"

Dr. Dix said, "Yes, of course. These are all simple operations."

Perlberg started for the door. "I'd rather not watch the rest of this."

"You'll stay," Karew told him.

"Miss?"

Lang Strayton stopped, looking back over her shoulder. "Yes, what is it?"

A small black man in a spotless two-piece white worksuit was standing a few feet from her on the night street. He'd apparently followed her when she left Blind Lemon's flat to walk down to the Sunflower Club. "Allow me to introduce myself," he said, grinning. "I'm Philip José Shamba, a roving reporter for *Timelife* Newsdiscs."

The blonde girl started walking again. "I don't really believe I'm interested in subscribing."

Shamba chuckled. "No, no, I don't wish to sell you anything. I simply want to interview you about the incredible event which took place on the Charles River earlier today." He caught up with her, walked along at her side.

"Incredible things are always happening in Black Boston." There were a few other people on the street, none that she knew, though.

"I'm alluding to the amazing rescue of the passengers of the excursion boat."

"Oh, yes, that. I didn't actually see much of that, Mr. Shamba."

"No need to be modest with me, no need to let my *Timelife* aura intimidate you," said Shamba. "I've already established the fact you were accompanying the fellow who performed the miraculous feat."

"Even so, I don't really wish to talk about it."

"What sort of attitude is that? There are twenty-six million Newsdisc users who'll love to see something about the astounding events of this day." Shamba gripped her arm.

"No, you'd better—"

"We'd also like to know, Miss Strayton," he said as he shoved her into a darkened doorway, "if, as we suspect, your companion was Ted Briar."

"You're not from *Time*—"

Shamba's stungun hummed. The girl fell back against the door.

The gray landcar, which had been following them at a discreet distance, rolled swiftly along the dark street to stop directly opposite the doorway.

Chapter 18

SUNLIT fields of yellow grass stretched in every direction. Beyond them rose gently rolling hills. Cottages with slanting thatch roofs dotted the fields, nestled in pools of deep shade provided by the sturdy trees. Birds sang in the golden brown branches, a drowsy stillness pervaded the midday landscape.

"I didn't quite hear your last few words," Ted told his escort.

"The entrance fee, to look around Utopia East, is seventy-five dollars," repeated the pleasant-faced old man who'd met Ted at the toll gates of the idyllic community and escorted him this far. "If you want lunch, too, it'll run you either ninety-five or a hundred and five."

"There's a choice on the lunch?"

"You get the tour of the community and the Pond Lunch for ninety-five, the Peak Lunch'll set you back a hundred and five."

"Pond or peak?"

"Seemingly you're not familiar with the contemplation areas here at Utopia East," said the old man in the crisp two-piece walking suit. "If you care to contemplate a woodland pond while lunching, that's ninety-five dollars. Should you prefer contemplating on a mountain peak it's a hundred and five. We're running short on ponds today, so should that be your choice I advise you to sign up quickly."

"Not really that hungry. I guess I'll take the tour and skip lunch."

"Suit yourself." The old man held out his hand. "We accept Banxchex or multicards."

Ted produced the multicard he'd acquired this morning while en route to Utopia East. This time he'd telekinetically swiped one from a branch office of the multicard company. Standing, in the gray dawn, a block from the office, he'd caused the computer to print him up a new card in the name of Theo Bruin. Then he'd fiddled with the various other machines and mechanisms so that no one would be able to tell Theo Bruin hadn't existed until today. Should have done that in the first place, but you have to make a few mistakes before you get a new system worked out. He could stay at Utopia East as long as he cared to, provided the guided tour made the favorable impression Ted was fairly sure it would. TSA would never be able to find him. "Yes, here's my card."

The old man left him by a flowering bush, went trotting through the waving grass to the nearest tree. He thrust the card into a slot in the tree trunk, depressed several bark-colored buttons, and stood back to wait. After a moment a tiny speaker in the bole of the tree began to squawk quietly.

From the dustless road Ted couldn't catch any of the communication.

The old man glanced over at him several times before returning to the road. "Well, sir, you're in for a particular honor, young fellow," he announced.

"I only want the seventy-five dollar—"

"Turns out, and I should have guessed, you're exactly our one-hundredth visitor today," continued the gatekeeper of Utopia East, "meaning you are to be given a free special Honored Pilgrim Tour. Yes, and your guide will be none other than Dr. Norbert Perola himself."

"That's an honor sure enough, although—"

"Lo, he's fast approaching now."

Jogging along the road toward them was a huge man, his bald head flashing in the sun. He wore the same sleeveless tweed tunic and one-piece lycra worksuit Ted had become familiar with through his early-morning watching of the TV wall.

"Hi, chum," called Dr. Perola when he was yet fifty yards off. "Good to see you."

"It's an honor . . ."

"Never shake hands," explained the giant philosopher when he drew up in front of Ted. "Only salute, casually, like so. You're Theo Bruin, eh?"

"Named after an uncle," said Ted. Up close Dr. Perola seemed even larger than he did on the wall. "I'm interested in your community, Doctor, thinking of settling here for a bit."

"Smart idea, chum," said Perola. "Never slap on the back, but consider yourself warmly congratulated for your decision." He made a go-away gesture at the old man. "Back to your post, Fritch, and your meditations."

"Yes, as you say, Dr. Perola."

Dr. Perola asked Ted, "Tranquil here, isn't it?"

"Very much so, yes, which is one of the reasons I—"

"The invention of noises was yet another of so-called civilization's follies. Come along this way, Theo. Who needs noise, chum? Nobody really, yet many feel it's a necessary byproduct of progress. Not so."

The enormous Perola led him up from the main road onto a path which wound through the grassy fields. "As I was saying," said Ted, "the quietness here was one of the—"

"You'll be wanting lunch first."

"Not really. I—"

"We've all been led astray in the chow department, too, chum. People starving here, there, everywhere. Supposed to make us feel guilty. You sit down to a nice thick juicy texturized vegpro steak smothered in synonions and gluten gravy and you're supposed to feel ashamed. What about all those poor slat-ribbed jigs over in someplace I never heard of? What of those skinny, sad-eyed greaseballs down in some smelly South American country not worth the powder to blow it up? Well, they can go farb themselves. No reason why they couldn't have figured out how to fill their bellies as good as us. No reason they couldn't invent a tangy ice-cold bottle of nearbeer instead of standing around rattling their cup for a handout. That reminds me, we'll have ice-cold nearbeer with our lunch. Right in here.'' They'd arrived at a cottage, the door stood a few inches open. Dr. Perola booted it wide with one of his enormous feet.

"Be okay with me if we see your setup first and then—''

"Plenty of time after we tie on the feedbag, Theo.'' The parlor of the cottage was blue, with blue walls, blue rugs, blue furniture, blue light mobiles. "Everything's been color-coordinated, helps you relax.''

Two places were set on a blue table.

A blue door swung open, admitting a blue serving robot. "Two tangy ice-cold bottles of nearbeer,'' it said, bobbing its ball-shaped head in the direction of the blue tray it was carrying. The robot rolled to Ted.

"I'm not really thirsty.''

"Take one, chum. We'll drink a toast to your arrival at Utopia East.''

"Well, okay.'' Ted allowed the blue robot to unzip a bottle and pour it.

"Don't believe in clicking glasses,'' said the philosopher, "but you can take the word for the deed. Bottoms up.''

Ted drank half of his nearbeer, set the glass on the blue table. "I've watched your show, Doctor," he said. "I don't think, though, you've ever mentioned what exactly the rates are here."

"We have several plans, chum, several plans. The basic weekly rate is six-hundred dollars, which doesn't include any frills. You get a pallet on the floor, breadsub, neowater, a . . ."

Ted noticed the room was changing color, sliding from blue to green. A very nasty green, glaring, yellowish. He blinked, the green darkened. "I'm . . . I . . ."

"Feeling poorly, Nemo?"

"You . . . you're . . ."

"Right you are, chum. You are directly atop a Total Security Agency installation. Once you conk out from the micky in your brew I'm going to haul you down there so they can get to work on you. You don't think you would have watched my nerd of a show of your own free will? It was programmed into you when—"

"No, I'm not going . . . not going to stay here."

The huge doctor approached the swaying Ted. He opened his arms, grabbed him in a powerful hug. "Don't like touching people, but I'll make an exception. You're too far gone to pop off, chum."

Ted's fists clenched. "I am . . ." He concentrated, trying to will himself out of there. Minutes drained away, the room grew black, he remained in the grip of Dr. Perola. "No, damn it, you're not going to keep me here!"

The air exploded, the philosopher found himself hugging nothing.

   * * *

"Oops!"

Hundreds of tiny American flags went falling from the work table, flapping and fluttering like a huge flock of patriotic butterflies.

"More sabotage?" inquired old Woodruff, who'd been sitting on a stool with a plyoflask of brandy resting on one star-spangled knee.

Moriarty, the lanky nineteen-year-old TSA agent, had materialized a few inches from the work table in the old man's office. Before he could stop himself he had fallen against the table and upset the enormous stack of new breakfastburger premiums. "Excuse me, sir," he said, "I seem to be in—"

"Give the people patriotic food and you have to expect sabotage," said Haley's father after a swig of the flask. "I'm, by the way, taking this brandy for medicinal purposes. In hopes of preventing some fatal respiratory complaint. I was recently up a flagpole."

"Mrs. Seuss was so certain he was here," Moriarty said mostly to himself. "Go down there and you'll find Ted Briar." He bent, starting to gather up the little fallen flags. "Shows you can't trust somebody who looks like Milton Watcher's mother, especially—"

"You just mentioned the name of my vicious lout of a son-in-law, didn't you?"

Moriarty straightened. "You know Ted Briar?"

"Alas, to my sorrow," replied Woodruff after another swig. "He's married to my only daugh-

146

ter. A lovely girl, who was destined to be one of the country's great dancers until this lump came along to chain her to the rock of—"

"Has he been here lately?"

"How do you think I got up the damn flagpole? I saw him grinning up at me, and I know he had something to do with it."

"When was this?"

"I'm not exactly sure. The shock of flying from that pole has somewhat disoriented me."

"You wouldn't know where he went, sir?"

"Off to break someone's heart, probably my gifted daughter's." Woodruff, hitching up his Uncle Sam pants, left the stool to walk closer to Moriarty. "You look like a nice-enough, although incredibly clumsy, young man. I imagine you're dutiful to your parents." The old man stroked his beard, which was pasted to the left side of his neck. "You're looking for Ted, are you? Would that be in some legal capacity?"

"I'm not at liberty to say, sir." He returned his attention to collecting the scattered flags.

"You have my heartfelt best wishes in your quest. I hope you find him and see he gets what he deserves."

"Oh, I'll find him all right," promised Moriarty.

Chapter 19

THEY were all thin, except one. They stood in the jigsaw afternoon shadows thrown down on the ruined street. The heavy-set young man was out in the hazy sunshine, hands on hips, lips puckered, and whistling almost silently.

"Long Island," said Casper to Reverend Ortega.

The priest continued to hand out the food packets, one of protein meal, one of neowheat flour. "That's my impression of him."

"Bless you, Rev," said the next woman in the Gramercy Park food line.

"And bless you as well, Mrs. Trego."

"One of the Suffolk guerrillas, you think?" Casper lugged another carton of food packets out of their landvan.

"He's not the guy they usually send, but probably. Most of them tend to swagger out that way.''

The quietly whistling young man rubbed his palms on the legs of his yellow trousers. Winking at them, he came walking out of the sunlight to the priest and Casper.

''Can't you see there's a line?'' a thin old man asked him.

''You needn't fear me, sir. I'm not here to take your food from you, nor to spy on you for the Roamers. I have business with Rev O.''

''We'll be finished here,'' Reverend Ortega told him, ''and moving on in a few minutes.''

Casper asked him, ''What's your business exactly?''

''I'm from Long Island.''

''That's obvious.''

''You both know who sent me,'' said the fat youth. ''I've got some important information for the Rev.''

''After the food is distributed, I can listen to what you have to say.''

The young man smiled. ''I'll hunker myself down on the curb to wait. Came over to introduce myself so you wouldn't become worried.''

''We weren't worried about you,'' said Casper.

The edges of the day were giving way to twilight when the last of the food was handed out.

''That distraction we had staged for the Roamers seems to have worked pretty good,'' remarked Casper.

"So far." The priest signaled the lookout men at each corner and they wandered away. To the fat youth from Long Island he said, "I can talk to you now. Who are you?"

"My name is Totter." He opened his hand to reveal the green neoglass marble he was holding. "This should identify me."

The priest plucked the marble off Totter's palm, rotated it between his fingertips. "All right, hop in the van. We have to move on." He climbed in, sat on the floor among the empty food cartons.

Totter followed him in, Casper shut the doors on them and hurried around to take the wheel of the van.

"Something pretty large has come up," began Totter.

Reverend Ortega nodded his head. "Tell me about it."

The fat youth sat cross-legged, palms resting on his knees. "You know we have very good contacts with Brazil," he said as the van began to roll, "contacts with the guerrilla forces down there. In fact, one of our boys was just down there. You know him, Furtado."

"Furtado got into Brazil?"

"Yes, he got in and he was able to talk to the pro-Brazil leaders, including Francisco Travessa," said the smiling young man. "Furtado got back out again, back to Suffolk County. Travessa gave him a detailed report on some of the things our United States Military Force people are actually doing down there . . . including documentation on the use of nerveguns and some kind of germ-carrying missiles. In other words, proof that President Hartwell is helping the Brazilian government violate the Geneva Guidelines. Furtado was even able to bring back tri-op film of the weapons in actual use, and a lot of photos of the victims.''

Reverend Ortega said, "I'd like to see that stuff.''

"We figured you would, which is why Furtado sent me in to contact you,'' said Totter. "He wants to meet with you tomorrow morning. Because TSA may have a hint of his trip and what he brought back, Furtado couldn't risk coming into Manhattan himself.''

"What time tomorrow?''

"Can you be at our Shantytown place at six A.M.?''

"Yeah,'' answered the reverend. "Can Furtado turn some of this material over to me?''

"Exactly what he wants to do.''

"I'll be there.''

Getting to his feet, Totter said, "Tomorrow at six then. Can you drop me off now?''

Ortega called to Casper, "Stop the van.''

When they were moving again through the dusk, and Ortega was up in the passenger seat, Casper said, "I don't like that fatass guy much.''

"You don't have to like him,'' said Reverend Ortega. "With the stuff Furtado's got, and what Ted Briar will eventually bring us, we'll have enough to finish Hartwell and his administration.''

"Maybe, but—''

The blind-phone on the dash buzzed. Ortega flipped the answer switch. "Yeah?"

"News from our New Westport man," said a girl's voice. "It concerns Nemo's wife. I believe you'll want to do something about it."

"We'll be back at the mission in ten minutes," said Ortega.

Chapter 20

". . . NOT the right word . . . getting closer, Will, my lad, although it's not the proper word . . . Let's see now . . . Go back over what you've got . . . *My Deck, a Poem by Will Gump* . . . So far, so good, Will, my lad . . . *A bridge taking no one anywhere* . . . Perfect so far . . . Exactly right . . . *A bridge taking no one anywhere . . . A compilation of neowood serving only* . . . Nope, nay, your artistic instincts are as accurate as ever, Will, my lad, and you realize, quite rightly, *serving* isn't the proper word at all . . ."

Oil. Harsh-smelling oil, and thickly sticky. The smell of it all around Ted, the stuff adhering to the front of him.

" . . . *compilation of neowood trod by* . . . No, that lacks the vernacular Will Gump touch . . ."

The oil was spilled on the floor, on the planks

Ted was sprawled out on. It had soaked into the neowool blanket, seeped in between the cracks and joinings. The odor was swirling all around him.

Darkness, too. It was dark in this gently rocking place. Could it be night so soon? It was early afternoon when Dr. Perola had tried to get hold of him.

"... *My Deck, a Poem by Will Gump* ... Admirable so far ... Destined, if not in this benighted century, then in the next, to be one of the finest of the poems in my Houseboat Sequence ..."

Ted pushed with his hands at the oil-smeared floor. He got his head lifted above the planks. There was the moon over there, but bobbing up and down. "Don't look, it'll make you dizzy again." He closed his eyes.

"... *bridge taking no one* ... Splendid, Will, my lad ... *no one anywhere* ... A powerful image, a brilliant notion in comparing this deck of my beloved old houseboat to a bridge ... No matter that few will see the parallel ... The last century was benighted, this one is ... Wait, Will, my lad, be patient ... The next century will be better ... bound to be ..."

"Hey!" Ted had his head raised, eyes open again. "Can you help me out?"

"Soon as I have found the precise word."

Ted could see him now. An old man in a canvas chair, a very old man, covered with tangled white hair. White hair which flowed from his scalp, sprouted from his ears, cascaded down from his

154

hidden chin. The old man's lumpy hands, clutching a talkwriter, were rich with mats of white hair, little tufts of it decorated his puckered elbows. His skin, what showed, was a leathery weathered brown. Above his ancient head the orange-streaked moon bobbed.

"On a ship," Ted decided. "I'm on a ship. Hey! Is this a ship?"

". . . *bridge taking no one anywhere* . . ."

"How'd I get from Utopia East to this boat?" Another push toward the tilting planks brought Ted to his knees, one more and he was upright, though shaky. "I was in enough control to teleport away from Perola. I can't remember where I wanted to go. Hey, excuse me, is this your boat?"

The very old man scowled across the deck at him. "Like all the rest, you have apparently never heard of my Houseboat Sequence of poems, nor of me, the immortal poet, Will Gump."

"No, I haven't," admitted Ted. "I don't seem to have much time for reading anymore."

" 'Twas the same in the twentieth century," sighed the old poet. "Same in the nineteenth century, for that matter. Ignore Will Gump, make a fuss over his inferiors, pass him by when it comes time to pass out the awards and the honors. Give the Pulitzer to this effete hack, heap Nobels on that tongue-tied buffoon, and all the while ignore Will Gump. I vowed I'd win a Nobel before the twentieth century was over . . . and here it is twenty blasted years into the twenty-first."

"This is Long Island Sound, isn't it?" Ted had been able to reach the railing.

"You've obviously never read my Sonnet Sequence based on objects found floating in the waters of the Sound."

"No, I'm afraid not. Sure, there's the New Westport Yacht Club right over there, I recognize the lights now."

"Will Gump has dwelled here for decades," said the bearded old man, "and they haven't named one single street in Westport after me, not even a little twisty lane."

"When I started to pass out I must have meant to come back home, to Haley," said Ted. "I thought of her first when I was in trouble. Which indicates I must—"

"May I suggest you cease mooning about and disembark, I have a major poem to get at."

"Sorry, am I keeping you from your deadlines?"

"Will Gump doesn't have deadlines. I write for the ages. Possibly not for this century, possibly not even for the next."

Ted studied the poet's face. "You mentioned, a bit back, the nineteenth century. Surely you—"

"Will Gump was born in 1855," the old poet said. "I've been waiting ever since for recognition."

"You mean you're a hundred and sixty-five years old?"

"And ignored by your emasculated literary pundits for every blessed year of that time."

"Even now people don't live anything like that long, Mr. Gump, not as flesh and blood anyway," said Ted. "If you really have some knowledge about how to prolong life, you ought to share—"

"Screw the rest of them, I'm only interested in keeping Will Gump alive. Enough competition as it is. Get Tennyson safely buried and up pops Vachel Lindsay and then you no sooner—"

"If you're a hundred and sixty-five years old and can prove it, you can be famous merely for that. You don't have to write any poetry at all to get people to pay attention to you."

Will Gump laughed. "The adulation of the mob isn't what I'm seeking. Anybody can be famous if he wants to cheapen himself. Will Gump will be honored for his real achievements or not at all."

Ted had begun pacing the deck. "How long ago did I . . . arrive here?"

"What does that have to do with Will Gump's poetry?" inquired the old man. "I was polishing the title of my latest when I noticed you for the first time. I labored on that title, wrestled with it, from high noon until two or three."

Ted consulted his watch. "Nearly ten now. That stuff Perola slipped me was pretty effective."

"All this gab brings us no closer to your departure."

"I'll be doing that in a—hey!" Ted suddenly had a picture of Lang Strayton inside his head.

157

"Something . . . something's wrong. I've got to go back to Black Boston first. Lang's in trouble . . . trouble with TSA."

"Let me not detain you."

"Yeah, before I can see Haley, I'll have to find out about Lang," Ted said. "Thanks for letting me sleep on your deck, Mr. Gump."

" 'Twas simpler than wasting poetry time to drag you to the rail and deposit you in the waters of the Sound."

"Thanks anyway." After a nod at the old man, Ted disappeared from the deck.

Gump leaned back in his canvas chair. "*My Deck, a poem by Will Gump,*" he said.

> "Some got six months, some got a solid year.
> Some got six months, some got a solid year.
> But me and my buddy doin' lifetime here."

Philip José Shamba gave a mock shudder. "How I loathe that last-century spade music," he said. His white tunic hung on a wall hook, his white trousers were stained with red splotches.

"We need the music to muffle the noise," said the wide, low-browed man who was holding Lang to a lucite tubechair.

The girl was unconscious, head dangling far to the left.

This musty loft was at the edge of the Black Boston blues district. The three speakers mounted on the beams of the ceiling were broadcasting a session from a nearby club.

"I wonder do my good gal know I'm here.
I wonder do my good gal know I'm here.
If she do, she sure don't seem to care."

"Rhyming here with care, that's very quaint,"
said the black Shamba as he approached the girl.
He raised her head by grabbing her hair, then he
slapped her again across the cheek. "What do you
know about Ted Briar? We know you were travel-
ing with him. Where is he?"

"She's still out," said the wide man. "Come
on, Shamba, we got authorization to use talkdrugs
on this one."

"Drugs," said the little man, letting go of
Lang's hair. "I've no need to rely on artificial
aids. I can persuade anyone to talk, with no more
than my hands *and* my mind."

"She's not going to talk this way. We're going
to end up with another stiff, like that time in
Providence. I'm not going to fake another—"

"One thing I don't require from you, Pritchard,
is advice. Our relative positions in TSA ought to
show you which of us is the most highly valued."

"Pulling rank doesn't scare me, Shamba,"
Pritchard said. "I don't think you ought to hit her
anymore. We're going to use the . . ." He
frowned, glanced around the room. "What just
happened?"

"Nothing."

"Yeah, it . . . the music all of a sudden quit."

"Probably those howling idiots are taking a
rest." Shamba got hold of Lang's face in his
hand, applying pressure to her cheek bones.

"Stop faking, Miss Strayton. Tell me where Ted Briar is!"

"Right here."

"Oh shit." Pritchard backed away from the tube chair.

"You I don't need," Ted told him.

The wide Total Security agent disappeared from the loft.

Shamba released his hold on the girl, turned to face Ted, smiling. "This is much more than I hoped for." A hand moved toward his waistband.

Ted stepped in close, slapped him across the mouth. "Is it? Good. I don't like what—"

"Idiot!" The black man thrust a leg between Ted's, levered him by his left arm.

Ted slammed into the wood floor.

"You may think you're an agent, Briar, but you're no fighter." Laughing, Shamba kicked Ted in the chest as he attempted to get up.

Ted half rose, stumbling, fell against a wall. "I can handle you without using any—"

Shamba kicked him again, this time in the tailbone.

Ted smacked into the wall, dropped flat out.

The little TSA man dived on him, hitting hard into his back with both sharp knees. "You haven't a chance in the world, my friend."

As he struggled to get control of himself, Ted realized his original idea of fighting Shamba hand-to-hand wasn't going to work. "So much for fair," he muttered.

Shamba twisted both hands into Ted's hair,

commenced to drum his head on the planking again and again.

"Got to send you some . . . someplace else." The slamming of his head continued, continued. "Someplace else."

It stopped.

Ted attempted to move, found no one on top of him. With a very painful pushup motion he reached his knees. "I'm really . . . going to have to . . . get over these notions . . . about fighting fair." Finally he made it to a standing position.

Lang had toppled from the chair during the fight with Shamba. She lay, sprawled and limp, on the loft floor.

Ted ran, as best he could, to her and got an arm behind her shoulders. "Lang, hey, Lang."

"Don't," she said in a faraway voice, "know anything."

"It's me, Ted. I'm sorry they—"

"Oh, I'm happy to see you again, Ted. I really expected we'd never meet again. People always say they'll keep in touch, but that rarely works out."

He smiled. "You're recuperating."

"Because I'm able to talk in my usual fashion? Yes, I suppose that is a good vital sign." With his help she sat up. "Did you get rid of the pair of them? They were, especially the one in the white suit, certainly anxious as to your whereabouts."

"Yeah, they're out of the way for awhile, a good while," Ted assured her. "I didn't expect they'd come after you, must have traced one of those damn cards I swiped."

"They want you very much, Ted. If they did this to me . . . You have to get to your wife. They might—"

"That's my next stop, Lang. I just all of a sudden got a flash you were in trouble up here."

"That was a true flash all right."

"Okay now," he said. "I've already talked to your friend Lemon, before I showed up here. He'll be able to look after you. TSA probably won't send anyone else to question you."

"Yes, and you'd better . . . teleport or whatever it is to your wife," suggested the girl. "But first . . ." She put, gingerly, her arms around Ted and kissed him.

Chapter 21

HE arrived. There he was in a stand of decorative trees near his house. "Something . . . something isn't quite right around here," Ted told himself as he stood there on the night street. Not moving, he studied his house. Lights showing, nothing unusual.

"Yeah, that's it. They haven't got anybody watching the place." Ted was certain of that. Nowhere, not within a square block of his house anyway, were there any Total Security agents. "What's it mean?"

Someone in the house. It was Haley, Ted sensed that. "She's alone, too."

Nobody watching for him outside, nobody waiting inside.

"Unless they're counting on her letting them know if I turn up. No, Haley wouldn't do that. She might sleep with that nerd Perlberg, but she wouldn't hand me to TSA."

Besides, the Total Security people knew he was capable of teleporting her out of the house if he chose.

"So why aren't they more worried?"

Somewhere inside his head a hunch was trying to form, a sensing of why the agency could afford to let his wife sit there in their house unguarded and unobserved.

"Something electronic . . . is that it?"

Ted wanted more time. To watch his house, to think this out, to develop his hunch. He was still getting used to his abilities. He'd been feeling that some of the hunches he'd had lately were linked in with his extrasensory abilities.

"Wally," he thought. "I can trust Wally Klennan. Sure, he's one of the few friends I've got hereabouts."

Ted was standing in the unlit recroom of the Klennan house. From the unblanked window he could see the front of his home. "Looks too normal, everything is too normal."

Ted moved to the doorway, listened. Connie's voice from the kitchen. Talking with Wally? No, she was complaining to the house computer about something.

". . . flasks all spotted."

"This is a hard-water area, ma'am. We haven't yet found a . . ."

Wally's house had a much pleasanter voice, was a hell of a lot politer, too.

"Ted!"

Wally had come around a bend in the corridor.

"I don't know if you know what's been going on, Wally, but—"

"Get back in there." His friend pushed him into the recroom. "Let me blank the windows. There."

"Wally, I—"

"One more thing first." From a tunic pocket he took a tiny silver bubble. After bringing it close to his eyes, Wally said, "No eavesdropping gear in here."

"Why would anyone want to listen in on you? You mean because you know me?"

Shaking his head, Wally replied, "I'd better tell you who I'm really working for, Ted."

Running his tongue over his suddenly dry lips, Ted said, "You're not with the Total—"

"Do I look like a TS agent?"

"I don't know. Lately . . . I'm not sure who anybody really is. Turns out my early-morning hero, Dr. Perola, is a TS man."

"I could have told you that," said Wally. "I'm working with Reverend Ortega."

Ted said, "So you told him about the TF session, about my dream, lifting the damn machine and all?"

"Yeah, I've known for several months about your career as Nemo, but—"

"You could have let me know that."

"Ortega didn't think you were ready back then."

"Jesus, the way people go around making decisions about me, about my life."

Wally put a hand on Ted's shoulder. "There's something more important I have to tell you," he said. "We can, hopefully, go into the details of some of this other stuff later. You came back on account of Haley, didn't you?"

"I decided I wanted to see her, that I shouldn't have simply dumped her here. Maybe that's a mistake. She may want to go on like always with . . . You know about Perlberg?"

"Yeah, that, too."

"You might have mentioned at least—"

"Ted, listen. They got to Haley, did something."

"What do you mean? Did what?"

Wally said, "Perlberg set it up, came over here and used a stungun on Haley—take it easy and listen. Then a TSA team, headed by Dr. Dix, came in. I haven't all the details, but it involves implanting."

"They operated on Haley, hurt her?"

"This kind of implanting is painless, the subject usually doesn't even remember it was done. You ought to know . . . No, you wouldn't. I keep forgetting you've only been aware of—"

"What did they implant?"

"An alarm device with a tracker, whole gadget the size of a grain of rice. If you show up over there it'll warn them, and if Haley leaves, on her own or by way of teleportation, they're alerted and can pick up her exact location no matter where she's gotten to."

"That's not," said Ted, "really so bad."

"Well, no . . ."

"That's not all they did though, is it? Something in your voice. What else?"

Wally moved to the blanked window. "This one I don't have the details on," he said. "But it's . . . a microminiaturized bomb."

Ted went striding to him. "What are you talking about?"

"Total Security's had these things for a couple of years. A bomb, no bigger than your fingernail, which can be implanted. There are, far as Reverend Ortega's been able to find out, several varieties. One which works along the lines of a traditional time bomb and explodes a given number of hours after its planted. Another type, more sophisticated, can be activated at any time they want."

Ted said, "Since they want to get me, what they've used on Haley must be the one they can set off at will."

"You've got to remember that TSA probably wants you alive, Ted. This bomb thing is just extra protection, maybe something to use to bargain with you," said Wally.

"They'd kill me as a last resort."

"Rather than allow you to keep running free, yeah."

"Okay, suppose I simply remove their gadgets? Use my telek powers to take them out of Haley's body?"

"Since they don't expect you to know about the implanting, it's possible you can do that," said Wally. "But it's also possible the removal will set off an alarm or . . . maybe even cause the bomb to go off. I'm sorry, Ted, that I haven't been able to find out more about the specific type of gadgets they've used.''

"Dr. Dix knows. You said he was in charge of what they did to Haley.''

"Sure, obviously, he knows. But it's not safe for you to—''

"He'll tell me.''

"Ted, you'd better not try to get to him.''

"Don't worry. Ted Briar they might be able to stop, but not Nemo.''

Before Wally could say anything further, Ted vanished from the room.

Chapter 22

"I NEVER thought much about aging before." Jay Perlberg studied his reflection in the chrome surface of the monitor machine. "Now I detect wrinkles, ravages of time. We shouldn't have done anything to Haley."

Dr. Dix was dictating into the voicehole of the talkwriter on the floating lucite desk in front of him. ". . . final stage of Reverend Ortega, alias Rev O, removal procedure will occur at six A.M. tomorrow. The renegade cleric has fallen for the subterfuge completely, and will show up in Shantytown at dawn fully expecting to be handed a bundle of damaging antigov material. He will instead meet poor obese Totter, who believes he is a rising young Total Security double agent and not simply the walking bomb we know him to be. Yes, once again—"

"You've become very fond of implanted bombs," said Perlberg as he stretched the tan skin beneath his left eye with a forefinger. "Nobody's safe."

"Perhaps you have one up your ass." Dix looked up from his dictation.

Automatically Perlberg patted his backside. "Your sense of humor is growing increasingly gross."

"Too much contact with the likes of Chief Agent Karew," replied the doctor. "None of you, I must say, truly appreciate the potential of my baby bombs. If we could implant one in every complaining antigov nerd in America we wouldn't have any more worries. Stay in line or . . . boom! That's a message even a fanatic can understand. Very humane, too. After the first few booms everybody would stay in line."

"That's a rotten idea," said Perlberg. "What you're doing already is rotten enough, but—"

"President Hartwell didn't take that view at all." Dix relaxed in his chair. "I'm a little concerned about you, Jay. You've been bitching and complaining a good deal of late."

"Spare me the veiled threats, Dix. I'm as loyal to TSA as you are." The handsome agent crossed to consult the dials of the machine which was monitoring Haley. "You got Karew to agree with you about doing what you did to Haley Briar. That doesn't mean I have to approve of any of it. While you may have the ear of the president, though that seems doubtful, I have several supporters on the Central Review Board. They're not as inhuman—"

"Jay!"

Perlberg had left the floor. He went rocketing straight up to the ceiling. His head smashed against the metal ribbing a half-dozen times, a half-dozen more. He plummeted down, slammed into the floor, went limp and unconscious.

"Now we can have a talk, Dr. Dix." Ted appeared next to the sprawled Perlberg.

"Ah, Nemo, so you've decided to—"

"Don't move, don't touch anything," warned Ted, "or I'll rip your heart right out of your goddamn body and stomp on it."

"I suppose you could at that."

Ted said, "I was out in the corridor a few minutes before I came in. What are you planning to do to Reverend Ortega?"

"Nothing at all, Nemo. What you apparently overheard was—ah!" Dr. Dix clutched his chest.

"That was just a little telekinetic tug on your heart, Dix. Don't bullshit me."

Dr. Dix slumped, massaging his chest and ribs, his pale face flecked with perspiration. "Reverend Ortega is going to be killed at six A.M. tomorrow in a place called Shantytown. It's almost directly across Long Island Sound from here." He stopped talking, to concentrate on his breathing. "A young idiot named Totter has a bomb implanted in his carcass. It's set to go off as soon as the reverend is within two feet of Totter."

"Does the one you put in my wife work the same way?"

"Nemo, my boy . . . No, the bomb used on Mrs. Briar has to be activated from here." He nodded at the monitoring machine. "You must understand that in your case it isn't part of any assassination plan, Nemo, but rather a safeguard in case you—"

"I want to remove it, and the alarm."

"You've learned a good deal about what are supposed to be clandestine operations. Might I ask—"

"I want to remove it!"

Dix wiped his forehead with his palm. "The surgical procedures are relatively simple, requiring not more than an hour."

"What happens if I take them out with my telek powers?"

After a second Dr. Dix answered, "I hadn't thought of that. Yes, I suppose that's perfectly possible."

"There are no extra safeguards? If I take the bomb out my own way it's not going to explode?"

"No," Dix assured him, "you won't have to worry about that."

"We won't have to worry."

"Eh?"

Grabbing the lank doctor by the arm, Ted said, "You're coming along with me."

"That's not—"

"But it is."

"Ted!"

"And this is Dr. Dix," said Ted a second after they'd materialized in his living room.

"I don't think I know—"

"No, he fixed it so you wouldn't remember him."

Haley left the chair she'd been sitting in. "Ted, I'm glad you're back but I'm afraid I don't understand what's going on."

"You will. Right now Dr. Dix is going to stand by while I do something."

Dix was paler, the beads of sweat larger. "You're making your situation even more difficult, Nemo. When my absence is noted you'll—"

"Nobody'll notice for awhile. Perlberg's out cold, you're here. Nobody's even going to notice the alarm. It's signaling right now, isn't it?"

"Yes, Nemo, and there's a backup monitor in Chief Agent Karew's office."

"We have a few minutes."

Haley, very cautiously, took Ted's hand. "What's been going on, Ted?"

"Pretty near everything," he replied. "Okay, Dix, I'm going to remove your gadgets now."

Dix swallowed. "The surgical method might be—"

"Not enough time for that."

"Wait!"

"Why?"

"The bomb will go off if either of the devices is removed without the safety switch being thrown."

"Oh, so? Where's the switch?"

"You have to flip the red and the green toggle on the monitor machine back in my office."

Ted closed his eyes for a few seconds. "Okay, that's done. Is that it?"

"Yes, yes, it's safe now."

Ted eyed the pale doctor. He turned toward his wife, fists clenching. "There." He opened his left hand to reveal two tiny silver objects resting in his palm.

Dr. Dix bowed his head. "Point to you, Nemo."

Haley shook her head. "I hope this is all going to make sense to me eventually."

"It'll make—"

A new voice came out of the house speaker. "Briar, this is Chief Agent Karew. We're aware you're in the house and we advise you to surrender without attempting to escape."

"You'd better comply," suggested Dr. Dix.

Ted laughed. "Like hell!"

Chapter 23

"TEN of them," said Ted, "all around the house."

"How," asked Haley, "do you know that?"

"I just know."

Dr. Dix wiped his forehead once more. "By far the simplest thing," he said, "is to surrender here and now, Nemo."

Ted took hold of his wife's hand. "I'm not through yet, doing what I have to do," he told the doctor.

"We're unblanking your windows, Briar," announced the voice of Chief Agent Karew. "Which should convince you we're not fucking around."

Three TSA men could be seen out on the front lawn, each standing slightly hunched, pistol in hand.

"You'll be a fugitive," reminded Dix.

"Things will get much worse than they have been. TSA can manufacture some charges against you, fake a little evidence. That way we can see to it the Federal Police get orders to mow you down."

"Better do that right away," said Ted, "because the Total Security Agency isn't going to—"

"Briar, Mr. and Mrs. Briar! You know the rules about lawn parties! This is an outrage, I must say."

"Who the hell's the fruitbar in the fancy uniform?"

"All of you, you'll have to go back inside. The Way of Life Patrol doesn't allow this sort of thing. Mr. and Mrs. Briar, I'm ashamed of you! Aren't you ash—off!"

"Drag him over into the shrubs for now."

"What's the idea . . . striking a general in the WOL Patrol—oof!"

Haley said, "Poor Bill Beck, wrong time to be upholding our way of life."

"We'll come in unless you come out at once, Briar," Karew warned over the speaker. "Don't try to teleport yourself or your wife clear of the house, it will have disastrous results."

"He doesn't know the implants are gone," said Ted.

"We'll count slowly from ten down to one, Briar. Then you'll have to . . . oops!"

Something thudded up on the roof.

"That's Karew," explained Ted. "The rest of

your boys, Dr. Dix, I think we'll dunk in the Sound. First the batch right out there.''

The three men rose up off the lawn and went cartwheeling away through the dark sky.

"Now the rest of them."

Dix said, "You'll seriously regret—" The air popped, Dix was no longer with them.

"Ted, this is . . . I don't know exactly what it is."

"Don't worry, hold on to me."

Casper was on his hands and knees in the corner of the scrap-walled chapel room. "I hear you back in there, little friend," he was saying. "So why don't you come on out? You're either a mouse or a rat, we can use either one."

"Where's Reverend Ortega?"

The black young man shot to his feet, spinning. By the time he was facing Ted and Haley there was a stungun in his hand. "Showing off, is that it? Show up out of nowhere while I'm trying to coax a live animal out of that hole in the wall and try to scare me so—"

"I've got to see him," persisted Ted.

"He's got a rendezvous tomorrow morning, doesn't he? Six A.M. out on Long Island?"

The Negro scowled. "Nobody knows about that."

"You're wrong there, Casper. Total Security knows about it," Ted told him. "They set the whole thing up."

"It's a trap, huh? Yeah, I knew that fatass wasn't right." He walked, aimlessly, around the

177

back room of the Central Park chapel. "Damn, I don't even know where he is, the reverend. We're closing down this place today, moving again like we always do. I got no way to get in touch with him."

"You can always contact each other."

Casper tugged at his ear. "You're only starting, Ted, to understand the spy business," he said. "The priest business is even tougher to comprehend. All I know is every once in awhile Reverend Ortega likes to go off by himself, to think and to pray. That's where he is now, off somewhere all alone by himself. He'll probably go from wherever he is right to that farbing meeting. See, they've promised him a lot of stuff about what's really going on in Brazil. He's very anxious about this meeting."

"Okay, try to locate him anyway," said Ted. "I'll start at the other end, with Totter and Shantytown. I should be able to defuse him."

"Defuse?"

"One of TSA's more recent breakthroughs, an implanted bomb."

Inhaling sharply, Casper stared suddenly at Haley. "I just remembered," he said. "We got word TSA did the same thing to your wife. She's liable to—"

"No, Casper. I took care of it."

Haley leaned back against a neowood section of wall. "Ted, is that what you had in your hand? Were those bombs and were they inside me?"

"Nothing to worry about now, Haley, nothing."

"Never am I going to comprehend all of what's been happening," she said. "But I know you saved me from something fairly bad. After everything . . . you really didn't have—"

"Yeah, but I did."

Chapter 24

"No, I never knew any of that about you," said Haley. "I didn't even know Jay was an agent for this Total Security Agency." She was sitting, arms folded under her breasts, with her back against the trunk of one of the trees on the weedy hill above Shantytown and its stretch of gritty beach. "The only reason I got involved with Jay . . . well, I was mad I guess. Mad at you, at Brimstone, at the Repo Bureau, at myself. Mad."

Ted was close beside her, eyes on the cluster of improvised huts and shacks below. There were fifty or so ramshackle buildings, long since abandoned, built of the leftovers and remains of the past fifty years. Sheets of plywood, strips of ironsub, slabs of imitation marble, canvas banners, landcar doors, neowood planks, chunks of lucite, blocks of syncrete, antique billboards, skycar windows. The night darkness was commencing to thin, day was nearer. "I didn't know much about what was going on myself," he said. "Inside my head someplace I knew. The dreams, me walking around in a nightshirt, that was what they were about. I was sending messages to myself."

"You had all of these . . . powers all along," said Haley. "Maybe if we'd known, things wouldn't have gone as bad as—"

"You have to be stupid for awhile, everybody does, before you get a little smart."

Haley said, "I always thought Jay was somewhat fond of me. The agency, though, must have prompted him to approach me."

"Probably."

"Hey," she said.

"What?"

"It suddenly occurs to me that our life in Brimstone is all over," answered his wife. "Your job, our friends, the whole pattern of life we had. Not that I'll miss it, but what do we do from here on?"

"Something will no doubt occur to us."

Haley said, "Dr. Dix threatened you. Is it likely you'll be a fugitive, hunted and all?"

"No, because once I clean up this assassination attempt on Reverend Ortega I'm going to gather enough material to expose the Total Security Agency, President Hartwell, and anybody who happens to be standing too close."

"Will that work? Is public exposure enough?"

"I believe so, and Ortega does."

Haley glanced down through the imitation trees at Shantytown. "Almost six A.M. Since we couldn't locate Totter anywhere else, do you think he's down there now?"

"I've been getting hunches lately, about what's coming, about where things are." He shook his head. "As far as Totter goes, though, I can't . . . Wait. Yeah, I'm getting a feeling. He's down there now. Totter . . . and two other agents. Waiting."

"Total Security's going ahead with the plan," said his wife. "They didn't call it off because you found out."

"They don't know I found out. The only guy who knows for sure is Dix," said Ted. "I teleported him quite a way from here. He can't have even reached a place where he can communicate with TSA yet."

"What about Reverend Ortega? Maybe your friend Casper was able to stop him from coming here."

"My feelings don't tell me that. The reverend will be . . . Yeah, Haley, there he is. See him coming along the beach."

Down on the gray sand the lean, black-clad figure of the priest was moving.

Ted brought his hands together. "First thing is to get that bomb out of Totter." He shut his eyes, squeezing his fingers tight. "Those toggles over in New Westport are switched off. So, okay, we can lift it right out of—"

Wham!

Up through the arriving morning flew shatters of glass, wood, plastic, neowood, synglass, shreds of canvas, cloth, and paper. A broken jigsaw, spilling across the dawn. Smoke followed, gray and thick, speckled with soot.

"Jesus! This one was different. This one was different . . . had an extra trick to it." Ted brought his fists down again and again on his knees. "Damn, now I've killed . . . killed them . . . again . . ."

"Ted, Ted." Haley put her arms around him. "There's no way you could have known."

"I should have gotten the information out of Dix, instead of showing off and teleporting him to the Brazilian jungles. Three men dead, all three of them dead."

"Reverend Ortega's all right," said his wife. "See, he's getting up. The concussion of the explosion knocked him down."

Ted said, "Better go talk to him."

"Good morning, Ted," said the priest as he dusted sand from himself. "This is your wife, isn't it?"

"Yes, this is Haley," said Ted. "What just happened, it's my fault. I didn't take enough—"

"He saved your life," Haley told the reverend. "This wasn't a real meeting, it was a Total Security Agency trap."

Ortega looked from her to the smoking hole where Totter's shanty had stood. "I'm not as smart as I thought I was," he said. "I was convinced this was safe, everything checked out."

"They had a bomb implanted in Totter," explained Ted. "He, of course, didn't know that, thought he was setting you up for some other kind of TSA accident."

"It went off," said Father Ortega, "too soon."

"I was attempting to remove it, telekinetically.

183

But they had an extra safeguard against that, one I didn't know about. The instant I started it moving, the bomb went off.''

"If you hadn't been here," said Ortega, "it would have gone off anyway, and me along with it.''

"Yeah, I know, but—"

"I was really counting on the report on some of the illegal weapons we're using in Brazil," said the priest. "Too bad that was only bait for the trap.''

"I can get you that kind of stuff. The TSA file rooms over in New Westport are full of it.''

"You sure?''

"I was nosing around over there last night." He held out one hand in front of him, fingers spread wide. "Here, for a start." A thick sheaf of pink-tinted faxpaper materialized on his palm.

Ortega took it, read the title off the cover. " 'Biological Missile Use in the Mato Grosso.' That's terrific. 'Ultimate Security Clearance Required to Read Further!' ''

"Here, here are some more." More secret-file material of the Total Security Agency began to pop out of the air, dropping to the sand around Reverend Ortega's feet.

The priest grinned. "This is more than enough, Ted," he said, squatting, sorting through the documents and reports. "Roscoe never had the clearance to get near any of this. Now with what I've got here . . . soon as I get this to a few of my people and then get it broadcast across the country, the TSA is finished.''

Ted took a step back from the pile of material. "Let me know if I can help you with that end of things."

"Where will you be?"

Ted had taken hold of Haley's hand again. "Away for awhile, but I'll keep in touch. I've figured out all sorts of ways to use my abilities to communicate with people. For instance . . . well, I can go into that later."

Nodding somewhat absently, Reverend Ortega turned his attention again to the papers apread out on the dawn beach before him.

Ted and his wife walked to the water's edge. "I guess we can't see him from here."

"See who?"

"Oh, an immortal poet I met." Ted pointed. "His houseboat should be directly across the Sound from us."

"You said you were going away for awhile. Am I going, too?"

"Sure."

"Read this part here," said Ortega, "this second paragraph on . . ." The priest rose up, looked around him.

The beach was empty.

"Excuse me for stepping on your dog," said Moriarty. The young man had just appeared in the center of Mrs. Seuss's living-room area.

"I have a definite location this time," she said. "This is absolutely—"

"Too late, Mrs. Seuss. I only dropped in to tell you, in case you hadn't heard, that the Total

Security Agency is toppling down all around our ears. It was all over the news this afternoon,'' said Moriarty, sidestepping the dozing cyborg spaniel. ''I really thought I'd get Ted Briar, too, and bring him in. Except those tips you kept providing have been either too late or—''

''I see the two of them now,'' continued the seer. ''Yes, and I'm getting a very positive feeling about the location. Ted Briar and his wife, Haley, are in the West of this country.''

''We don't need to know anymore. I came to tell you, in case you—''

''It is California South. Yes, that's where they are.''

''So I'll be getting along, I guess. Before my folks start to wonder where I've gotten to.''

''Ted and Haley are walking along a golden beach. They stroll hand in hand along the sunlit shore, the blue waters of the calm Pacific making a vast border to the sun-drenched sand, the surf foam swirling up across . . .''

MORE EXCITING SF AVAILABLE
FROM BERKLEY